Lock Down Publications and Ca$h Presents

BACK IN BLOOD 2

Gift Of Revenge

Written By

LO-LIFE

First Edition 2026

Printed in the United States of America

Lock Down Publications
P.O. Box 944
Stockbridge, GA 30281
www.lockdownpublications.com

Like our page on Facebook: Lock Down Publications
www.facebook.com/lockdownpublications.ldp

Stay Connected with Us!

Text **LOCKDOWN** to 22828 to stay up-to-date with new releases, sneak peaks, contests and more…

Like our page on Facebook:
Lock Down Publications

Join Lock Down Publications/The New Era Reading Group

Visit our website:
www.lockdownpublications.com

Follow us on Instagram:
Lock Down Publications

Email Us: We want to hear from you!

Dedication

What's good y'all, after reading my first couple series, a lot of people got at me about their names not being mentioned. To be honest, sometimes it's just a slip of memory. I always say, if I don't get you on this one, I'll get you on the next.

To Cash and the Lock Down Fam., much love and appreciation for allowing me to paint my pictures on a great stage. For someone in my position, this opportunity is priceless.

To all The Guys on that "Freaky Ferg", who read my work and gave me constructive criticism. Y'all let me know, my shit is gas. Straight pressure! Snook aka Lil Antho., work clean young nigga and hold it down. My nigga Tyler LeBlanc aka, T.Y (Jelly). Naw, let me stop playing bro. Like you always say, "It's hard being TY." To my nigga Free World Earl aka EJ, "the one that stamps the tramps," stay up my nigga, they gone have to let you go one day, and when you do, make them pay for it. To Tito. (Waco). "Have no fear, Tito's here." Stop drinking all them sodas, my nigga. Brian Loud aka. B. Loud. Thank you for all that money you gave me, when I skint your ass up on them bets. LOL. Naw, for real, I ain't never seen a nigga gamble as hard as you do. To D. Rose and Korey G., I'm waiting on y'all to drop some material, so we can co-author something. No one's going to know how live y'all are, unless y'all show them. To X-Man: You got to let up off them niggas. It ain't like it used to be. Boss niggas don't sweat the insignificant. To Tego: I just want you to know, I will always be up one. To Jesse J.: The game's the same, so us Playas should never change. To my old celly Jersey aka Trip, you need to retire G, we're getting to old for this shit. To all my Hispanic patnas who fucked with the kid, the long way. Ernesto "Tito" Nino. (San Antone stand up) I haven't met to many that are actually who they say they are. You're one of them. Keep your head up G. Edgar: (East Dallas, stand up.) Remember, when you're good to the game, the game's good to you. And when you get something on the G, it ain't free, you paid dues for that. Rudy aka Turtle: I might never meet someone I beat as badly as I beat you in Spades. Lol. One of the realest guys I've come across. Ray Ray: I'll never forget the love you showed, when others turn me away because of politics. For that, you will always be able to pull up.

Now for the ladies. I've pretty much shouted out everyone. Except one. To Dorian A. Taylor, my very *special* friend, confidant, and much more. For years, we've downplayed how much you mean to me. Not anymore. Thank you for all those trips to come see me and those long talks on the phone. I don't think you'll ever know how much it means to me. To my extra son and daughter, Charlotte and Austin aka. Monster Flex Fly, I love y'all like my own. Thank you for bringing your mother joy, and never start it, but when it comes your way, *show that work!*

Well, like I always say, if I missed you this go round, I'll try and catch you on the next. My goal is to keep them coming and provide the world with authentic, elaborate, street literature. Until the next time, East up till my feet up. Bombs over Baggdad!

Prologue

He laid in the bed, watching her sleep. Never in a million years, would he have suspected this. If you would have told him his life would have turned out like this, he'd never believe you. Shit, he might have went in your mouth for assassinating his character. Still, here he was.

Her essence, still heavy on his lips. She tasted just as good as he thought she would. No, better! The only question now, what to do with her? He had plans to carry out. Wicked, demented plans. Not because he was an evil man, but because men had done evil to him.

He gave them loyalty, and they gave him abandonment. He kept it righteous, and they rewarded him with betrayal. Now, it was his turn. He wasn't a religious man, per se, but he believed in a being. One who balanced the wrongs and rights of those who played the streets. Some called it Karma. Where he was from, Karma was the little sister. He prayed to the big brother. The oldest in existence. The one they called The Game God.

Little did people know, The Game God was real, and he answered prayers. And his prayer, was for the Gift of Revenge. Now that he'd been granted that, he needed to make right the wrongs. Balance the scales. That was the promise he'd made.

As he watched her sleep, his forbidden fruit, he started to put together his plan. No matter what, he would not stop until they all felt, his Lord and Savior's Wrath.

Chapter 1

Rashard

With no time to grab my pole, I look around for some type of weapon. I spot an empty champagne bottle on the ground, scoop it up, and run toward their direction. I just pray I make it to her in time. *If they got straps, we might both be dead.*

Alison's screams slice through the night air, and I kick myself for putting her in this position. If she wouldn't have come out with me tonight, she wouldn't be going through this.

A few months back, I ran a play on this Crip nigga named Xavier. Hit him with some counterfeits and came up on a k-pack of Percs and some smoke. On my way out his apartments, some of his boys got the drop on me. Next thing I know, bullets flying through my whip. I barely made it out alive.

Honestly, I ain't even worried 'bout them pulling up since then. Too much other shit going on. I guess I forgot. Xavier's punk ass didn't.

He must've found out I'd be out tonight and sent some of his homies to lay in wait. Soon as I went to the restroom, they snatched Alison and manhandled her out the club. If she wasn't so drunk, she probably could've put up a better fight. But thanks to me, she was lit off a whole bottle of Ace of Spades.

"Please… somebody he—"

"Bitch, shut the fuck up, fo' a nigga split your shit out here!"

The voices get louder; I'm getting closer. I duck behind a minivan, crouched low, empty bottle gripped tight in my right hand. They're only two cars over. I can hear her struggling against dude's grip.

"Fuuuuck!" one of 'em yells. "This bitch just bit me!"

Smack! The slap echoes, no doubt leaving a handprint on her cheek. "Bitch, you gon' regret that. Soon as we get to the spot, Imma show you what you can do with that mouth." I need to move fast. If they get her in the car, I might never see her again. My grip tightens on the neck of the bottle. I duck walk toward the trio. Their backs are to me as they wrestle Alison.

When I'm close enough, I spring up, swinging the bottle hard as I can. *Bsshhh!* The thick glass shatters against the first dude's head. He stumbles into a parked car, face first, then drops. Out cold. The second dude releases Alison and charges me. I size him up quick, he's got me by at least fifteen pounds. I let him close in, then snap a quick jab to his face. His head jerks back, lip busted.

I back out from between the parked cars to get some room. We square up. He's taller, so I know his reach got me. He stutter-steps, fakes left, then cracks me with a mean hook to the jaw. My teeth clamp down on my tongue, blood flooding my mouth. I try to dip inside his reach, but he catches me with an uppercut that damn near lifts me off my feet.

I stumble, dazed. Before I can recover, he's on me, heavy hands raining down. My back hits the car frame. No room to move. I cage up and wait for an opening.

"Aaagghh!" he howls, dropping to the ground. Hands clutching the back of his head.

Takes me a second to process, Alison's standing over him, one stiletto in hand. Blood dripping from the spiked heel. The puncture wound in his skull leaking as he screams in agony.

I wanna grab her and kiss her right then, but we ain't got time. I snatch her hand. She's hopping with one shoe on.

"Hold up, hold up," she pleads. I stop, give her a second to kick off the other heel, then we make haste.

Once we're in the car and hitting the freeway, I can't hold it in. I start laughing like crazy. "I ain't know you had it in you," I clown.

She's still shaking from the adrenaline, looking like she's about to hyperventilate. I reach inside my center console, pull out a bag of White Widow, and toss it to her.

"There's a cigarillo in my glove box. Twist one up for us."

Alison does as told. Minutes later, she's got a crudely rolled blunt lit. I let her take the first four or five pulls before she passes it my way. I hit it twice, then hand it back.

From the corner of my eye, I watch her shoulders drop, posture loosening. The shakes stop.

"You know," I joke, "I had that nigga right where I wanted him. You ain't have to jump in."

She giggles. "Oh, so you was doing that Muhammad Ali thing… what they call it, Scope and dope?"

"Rope-a-dope," I correct. "And that's exactly what I was doing." I playfully snatch the blunt back.

She gets quiet. I know something's on her mind. When she speaks, her tone is low.

"Rah… what the fuck were they gonna do to me? I didn't even know them dudes."

Ain't no telling what they had in store for her. Niggas out here these days? Straight creeps. "You don't need to think 'bout that no more. Whatever it was, it ain't happenin' now. We good."

She looks up, eyes glazed. "Thank you so much, baby. You came through for me. All I was thinkin' was: *Where's Rah? I hope he comes for me…* and you did. I love you, baby." *Muah!* She kisses me on the cheek. I wasn't expecting that. They say near-death experiences make people say and do shit outta the ordinary. *What would she say if she knew I was the reason she was in that predicament to begin with?*

When I called her sister to pick me up the day, I got shot at by them Crips, Alison was the one who drove me back to the hood. Hopefully, she never puts two and two together. I don't even know what to say. I just grab her hand, kiss the back of it. A single tear slides down her cheek. She tucks her feet onto the seat, leans over, and lays her head on my shoulder while I drive us home.

Next morning, I wake up to her lips wrapped around my dick. That was three hours ago, and I'm still sore from the night before. "Wild" would be an understatement. I lay back, watching her give slow, sensual neck. Her mouth's so warm and wet around my piece, I damn near think I'm knee-deep in some pussy. My nuts start to bubble. I wrap her weave in my fist and start humping into her mouth. Her throat opens; I fill it.

"Ssshit," I hiss. Saliva drips down my shaft, around my balls, down my ass crack. She feels my nuts jump, my shaft twitch, and gulps me at a fevered pace. *Ghlup. Ghlup. Ghlup.*

I feel it coming. With her hair in my fist and my cock buried in her throat, I jerk and unload globs of creamy nut down her throat.

"Agghhh… fuuccckk… ssshit… whoooh!"

Alison keeps sucking my head gently until my balls are drained. Then she licks around my shaft, my inner thighs, peppers me with kisses all the way up my body until her lips meet mine.

"Damn girl, I'mma miss your ass," I confess.

She rises up so I can look her in the eyes. "Do you love me, Rah?"

Now, to be fair, I'm assuming she's about to head back to college. My thinking? Once she's back in school, she'll forget all about me and this "love" obsession. So, I indulge her.

"Of course I love you, Alison. You're my lil' schoolgirl."

She bites her lip like she's weighing a decision. I don't know how I know, but my face drops.

"You not thinkin' 'bout stayin', are you?" I ask.

A smile creeps across her face. She's glad I figured it out so she didn't have to work up the nerve to tell me. She nods with glee.

"Come on, Alison. No, no, no. You gotta go back to school. I'm not tryna be the reason you fuck up your scholarship," I try to reason with her.

"Rashard, I don't give a damn about playing volleyball. It's not for me anymore. I don't need a college degree to make a good living. You're a boss nigga, Rah, and I want you to teach me how to be a boss bitch." I can't believe what I'm hearing. *Great dick will make a bitch do dumb shit!*

On one hand, I wouldn't mind having this young bitch around. Her pussy's always wet and tight. Head game immaculate. I know if she's here permanently, a nigga's liable to put a baby up in her. And just like I told her sister Danielle, I ain't tryna have no kids right now.

Then a thought hits me, *I can put her to work.* Teach her how to set niggas up. With her, I could take my game to the next level. *Does she got what it takes?* Only one way to find out.

"Look, Alison… I want you to stay, I really do. But you gotta understand the game I'm in is dangerous. Plus, I'll be on the move a lot. I don't want you stuck in the—"

"Let me go with you. Teach me the game so I can be an asset, not a liability."

I almost laugh at how easy this is. I thought I'd have to work to convince her to jump in the game. Instead, I get to play the reluctant role.

"I don't know, Alison. This game takes nerves, discipline, dedication. You can't have a heart out here, 'cause a heart will get you killed."

She doesn't even hesitate. "I'm ready. Please, Rah. I've never loved a man like I love you. I want to be with you. Your highs are my highs; your lows are my lows. Whatever I need to do, I'll do it."

I act like I'm thinking it over, but the truth. I decided the second I realized her worth. What I'm really debating is, *Who Imma sic her on first?*

"Okay, Alison. But make sure this is what you really want, 'cause once you jump in, ain't no jumping out." She needs to understand, this is a one-way street.

"I promise, baby. I'm not going anywhere. I'm down to ride this out till the end," she says with conviction. Then I think about something. "What 'bout Chance? What's gonna happen with that situation?" I see it, the quick flash of regret. *She really got love for him.*

"Well… I'll have to tell him it's over between us," she says.

I don't want to risk him talking her into going back to school, so I suggest. "How 'bout this Imma get you a new phone. If you serious about us, then you ain't gotta tell him shit. He'll be a'ight."

It's clear she ain't feelin' that. Her and Chance been dating since her freshman year. She feels like she owes him an explanation. I can respect it but fuck all that. I need to know she's with me a hundred and thirty-seven percent. I demand total obedience.

I watch her wrestle with the decision. Finally, she grabs her phone and hands it over. *Good girl.* I scoop my jeans off the floor and slide it into the front pocket. We spend the next thirty minutes getting our morning sex out the way. As I'm stroking her insides, watching her make those sex faces, I think *I can't wait to unleash her onto the game.*

Kay

"Damn… what time is it?" I groan, peeling my eyelids open.

Ever since I left the County, Claudia and I been fucking like jack rabbits. Her pussy's so velvety soft, and that bad boy feels like a water balloon. I can tell she's a real Boss Freak, just been holding back, probably didn't wanna give me the wrong idea. She lifts her head, grabs her phone off the nightstand. *8:55 p.m.*

"Oh shit," she blurts, jumping outta bed and scrambling for her clothes. "Shit, shit, shit… where's my panties? My shirt?… Fuck!"

"What's going on, Claw?"

"I need to get home. Harrell gets off soon, I gotta have dinner ready." She's halfway into her skirt, already sliding her heels on.

"Where you want me to drop you off at?" she calls, still rushing.

I throw on my TDC shorts and shirt, the same ones I wore to the County on that bench warrant.

"Take me to my T-Lady's crib. I'mma spend the night over there, but first thing in the morning, I'm headed outta town. Remember, Claw… don't tell nobody I'm back."

"I got you, boy. I understand," she says.

I grab her by the face, forcing her to look me dead in the eyes. "I'm serious, Claw. No one can know I'm home," I stress, squeezing her jawline, gentle but firm.

Her body shudders before she replies, "Yes, daddy, I got you. No one will know."

The look in her eyes is pure submission. I kiss her lips, taste myself on her breath. As we finish getting dressed and head out, I reflect on how crazy life can be. Never in a million years did I think I'd be fucking my brother's girl. Shit, just a year ago, I didn't think I'd see daylight again, let alone breathe the fresh air of the free world.

The niggas I sacrificed for left me to rot in a cell, no letters, no deposits. I know they never expected me to come back either.

As we head east on I-10, I start thinking about Claudia. She's been the only one, besides my mom, to be there for me. If I'm honest, I care for her deeply. Shit, I might even love her. But she's married to my brother, and even though I can't stand that bitch nigga right now, he's still my blood.

When we pull up to my mom's crib, butterflies hit my stomach. While I was locked up, one of my biggest fears was not being able to see her on solid ground before she passed. I made myself a promise: *If I ever touched down, I'd cherish every moment with her.*

"Aight, I'll hit you up tomorrow and let you know where Imma be at," I tell Claudia as I hop out.

"You better," she says with a smile.

I shut the door and head up to momma's front porch. *Ding-dong.* It takes her a minute, but when she opens the door, the sun couldn't compare to the smile she's wearing.

"Heyyy, boo," she sings, wrapping me in a big bear hug. I breathe in her coconut shampoo and cocoa butter lotion. I know she just got off work an hour ago and probably fresh out the bath.

"Hey, momma," I greet her, feeling like a kid coming home from summer camp.

She takes a second to size me up. When I left, I was about two-twenty. Now I'm two-forty, all muscle.

"Boy, look at you, looking just like your daddy."

My pops been gone twenty-six years flat. Last time I saw him, he was swole, muscles on top of muscles. I thought he was a giant back then.

"Gone on, momma. Pops had me beat by at least fifteen, twenty pounds," I tell her.

She leans back, eyes me skeptically. "You sure 'bout that? Boy, let's go inside. I know you need some real food in your stomach."

We head in, and the nostalgia hits me. Nothing makes a man feel grounded like being at momma's crib. Everything's just how I remember. A sweet aroma drifts from the kitchen.

"What you cooking, momma?"

She smirks. "Chicken and dumplings. Your favorite."

My stomach growls. I hadn't even realized I hadn't eaten all day, well, unless you count pussy. *Those hours spent sexing Claudia got my appetite raging.*

"Bet," I say, heading toward the kitchen.

"Kay, what the hell you think you're doing?"

I stop, confused. "Getting something to eat," I say, like it's obvious.

"Not until you wash up. I'm not even gonna ask *who*, but I can smell a woman all over you."

If I was white, my cheeks would be red. Instead of denying it, I just head to my old room, grab some clothes and a towel, and hit the shower.

I wasn't expecting my mom to notice I'd already gotten some pussy. She knows Claudia was the one who picked me up from County, but she also knows I could've easily had her drop me off at another female's crib. After all, she didn't see who dropped me off. Ain't no telling what's going through her mind right now.

Standing under the showerhead, letting the water beat down my back, I pray my mom never finds out about Claudia and me. She's big on loyalty, especially when it comes to family. If she knew I was fucking my brother's wife, she'd probably disown me.

I finish rinsing off, get dressed, and head back into the kitchen. Mom's on the phone.

"Yeah, girl… the negro had the nerve to call me this morning talkin' 'bout he apologizes and can he make it up to me."

She notices me and puts a finger to her lips, signaling for silence.

"You know I will… come on now. Yeah, I know… I can't this weekend, I gotta go see Kody. His parole lawyer says he should make his next review. Girrrlll, of course. Well, Linda, let me catch up with you later, I gotta take care of something. No, bitch, nothing like that, with your nasty ass."

She laughs, hanging up on her best friend.

Before I can say anything, she throws up a hand. "No, I didn't say anything about you being home. I promised you I wouldn't tell nobody, and I haven't."

My shoulders relax as she keeps talking. "Even though I don't understand why you don't want folks to know, I respect your wishes."

"Thank you, momma. Eventually I'll let people know, just not right now."

She nods, and we leave it alone. We spend the next hour catching me up on hood gossip—Danielle being pregnant. She knows I'm dying to know who the father's supposed to be, so she tells me straight up she ain't got a clue. Then she fucks my head up telling me AD is wanted for murder—something about shooting somebody at Andrea's job. *Probably caught her sucking some nigga's dick,* I think to myself.

After dinner, I suddenly feel drained. She hugs me, kisses my cheek goodbye.

When I get to my room, I spot a cell phone on the bed. There's a note with a number taped to it. I power it on, grab my Bible, and find my old celly Hector's number. I dial.

"Hola?"

"Hey, Hect. Wassup?"

"Kay… celly?"

"Yeah, it's me."

"Aye, chinga! Where you? Mi come get."

"I'm at my momma's crib. Come scoop me up tomorrow," I tell him. I can hear the excitement in his voice. Feels good to know somebody other than my mom and Claudia's happy I'm home.

"Si, si... umm, what's location? Mi come tomorrow morning, yes?"

"That's a bet, bro. I'll text it to you now."

I hang up and type the address but hesitate before sending. It ain't just anybody you give your mom's address to. Even though I haven't known Hector as long as Rah and them, the trust I have for him beats theirs by far.

Once that's handled, I call Ms. Dean, then Ms. T. Both on the same type of time, wanting to be the first to suck and swallow my nut in the free world. I don't tell 'em Claudia already beat 'em to it. I just say I'll be out of town and hit 'em up soon. They hang up, low-key salty.

Lying in bed, I run the day back in my head. Honestly, I couldn't have asked for a better first day out. Day two? That's when it really begins.

I drift off with a wicked smile on my face.

Chapter 2

Claudia

"Come on, come on…" I'm sitting at the intersection, and this damn light feels like it's refusing to turn green. My head's on a swivel, scanning for any signs of police. There ain't another car at the intersection besides mine and a white Honda Accord idling behind me. My hands tighten on the steering wheel. Just as I'm about to say *fuck it*, the light flips green. I mash the gas and speed the rest of the way home.

As I pull up to the two-story, four-bedroom home I share with my husband in Cypress, I check the time again, *9:15*. Harrell usually gets off at ten and makes it home around 10:40.

We've been married five years. Met through a mutual friend, and after that first conversation, we hit it off. He's got everything I look for in a man… except one thing.

I hit the garage opener and wait for the door to rise. I still need to shower, cook, and make sure everything is laid out for him. Since we got married, that's been part of my daily duties, and I take it seriously. Harrell makes enough so I don't have to work if I don't want to, but I'm not the type to just sit around and do nothing. Especially since we don't have kids.

I pull into the garage, hop out, and rush upstairs into the bedroom. As I scrub his brother's scent off me, I'm surprised by how little guilt I feel. Don't get me wrong, I love my husband. But there's a part of me he doesn't know. A part I'm scared to show him for fear he'd be repulsed. The part of me that's inexplicably drawn to his younger brother… Kaydon.

There's something about Kaydon that tells me he can master the darkness inside me. I need to be conquered, desperately. I hop out the shower, throw on a robe, and head straight to the kitchen. I need something quick and simple: chicken spaghetti with peppers and onions, sweet cornbread, and I grab a bottle of Crown from the cabinet.

As soon as I'm done, the garage door opens. I glance at the camera and see Harrell pulling in. I make sure I'm at the back door to greet him with a kiss and a light squeeze of his dick.

"Damn, baby… I love when you greet me like this," he says with a smile.

"Was' up, dinner will be ready in about twenty minutes," I tell him.

He pats me on the ass before heading upstairs. My heart pounds. Even though I scrubbed good, I swear I can still smell Kaydon on me. Might just be in my head, but I pray Harrell can't smell what I can.

While he's upstairs, I set the table and fix his plate. My mind drifts, *what am I gonna do now that Kay's home?* The sex between us was mind-blowing. I showed him a little piece of my repertoire, and he didn't flinch. Every stroke proved he could master my body. Just thinking about it has me leaking. With nothing under my robe, I feel my juices slipping down my leg.

By the time Harrell's done showering and comes downstairs, his plate's set on the table with a glass of Crown and Coke beside it. He kisses me in appreciation before sitting down to eat. By all accounts, Harrell is a good man; no, a great man. A provider. Sweet, caring, but firm. *The way a woman wants her man to be.*

There's no real reason for me to step out on him, but if I don't feed my darker urges, I'll lose my damn mind. I sit next to him, listening to him recount his day while he eats. Then he asks, "What you do all day, babe?"

"Nothing. Picked up some things, but other than that, I just laid around all day." *If only he knew the half of it.*

Once his plate's clean and his glass is empty, I put his dish away and pour him another drink.

"Let's go to bed," I say, pulling him toward our bedroom.

I know he's tired as hell, so I give him slow, passionate head until he floods my mouth with cum. I let him relax, then go down on him again. Once he pops his load the second time, he closes his eyes and falls out fast asleep.

I get up, rinse my mouth, and catch my reflection in the mirror. I can't help but think about the deal I made with the devil to make all this possible. *I hope it's worth it.* The next morning, I wake up to find Harrell already up and ready for work. He works twelve-to-sixteen-hour shifts, leaving at 5:15 a.m.

Me? I'm at a prominent law firm and don't have to clock in until 7. I sit up in bed, watching my husband get ready. With that working man's build, Harrell is ruggedly sexy. Suddenly, a mental image of his brother shirtless pops in my head, Kaydon, chiseled to perfection. Simply put, the man's sculpted like a god. I remember what he looked like before he went in, and prison did him justice. I don't know how I'm gonna manage this. Now that I've had a taste of him, there's no way I can leave him alone.

"What time you coming home tonight, babe?"

He glances back, almost apologetic. "Same as last night. Tom got hurt, so they got a bunch of us filling in to pick up the slack."

I fake disappointment, exhale. "Damn, babe, I hope you can get back to your regular hours soon. I miss spending time with you. We don't even get to watch a movie and chill anymore."

He walks over, caresses my face. "I know, baby. It won't last long. But you know I do this for us."

"I know… it's just—" I stop myself. "You know what, don't worry about me. I'll be fine. I got your back, my love."

He smiles, reassurance in his eyes. Harrell loves me truly, I have no doubt about his fidelity. By all accounts, he's the perfect husband. After kissing me goodbye, he heads out the door.

Immediately, I grab my phone and log on to my social media. Kaydon told me he'd contact me through there until we found a safer way to talk. I see a new DM, it's him, sending his new number. I save it under a woman's name, then hit him back.

BearClaw69: *Get off at 5. Want to spend time? Hit me.*

With that done, I hop in the shower. Today is one I've been anxiously waiting for. I knew the day after Kaydon's release was gonna be interesting.

After dressing in my charcoal-gray Michael Kors business suit, I make it to the law firm at 6:50 a.m. Walking through the lobby toward the elevator, it feels like everybody's eyes are on me. I've been at Bayter Law Firm for a year and a half, long enough to know some folks, but not long enough for everybody to know me.

I ride up to the thirteenth floor. The lawyer I work for, Lance Meyers, likes his coffee and pastry ready by 7:30. Lance is a forty-four-year-old white man with thinning brown hair. His wife left him for a younger guy, and ever since, he's been chasing younger women. When it comes to sexual advances, he's overly aggressive, but he's also one of the best lawyers in the firm. Matter of fact, *he's* the one who got Kaydon home.

I came to him asking if he knew anyone who could help. He said he'd take a look at the file and let me know. Once he reviewed it, he approached me with a proposition. Not really believing he could pull it off, I agreed. Now that Kaydon's home, I've got a debt to pay.

I set up my station, then went to grab his coffee and pastry. When I walk into his office, his back is to me while he's mid-conversation. Sounds like he's talking to a client, going over strategy for their upcoming trial.

I try to set the plate and saucer down and slip out without being noticed, but Lance turns and holds up a finger, telling me to "hold on a minute."

I stand there patiently, waiting for him to finish. As soon as he does, a big smile creeps across his face.

"So, Mrs. Snow… I see your brother-in-law is home free."

"Yes, he is, Mr. Myers."

"Please… call me Lance. Or better yet, call me *Master.*"

There it is. My deep, dark secret. I'm the type of woman who loves to be dominated, abused, degraded. How could I ever bring that up to my husband, a man who handles me with velvet gloves?

When I approached Lance about helping Kaydon, he said he could get him home, pretty much guaranteed it. His price: three sessions with me as his sex slave.

When I heard his proposal, I damn near came on myself. *How could he know that's exactly what my body craves?*

Of course, I played indignant at first, eventually succumbing to his request. Now that Kay's home free, it's time to pay the bill.

"Yes, Master," I reply.

Lance stands, walks toward me until he's just a foot away. He pulls a card from his pocket and jots down an address.

"This Saturday at 8:17 p.m. on the dot. Not 8:16. Not 8:18. If you're a minute late—or early—you will be punished. Do you understand me, slave?"

"Yes, Master, I do."

"Good. Do you have panties on?"

I bite my lip. "Yes, Master, I do."

"Remove them immediately."

I hesitate for just a second. His office door isn't locked, anyone could walk in while I'm slipping them off. The thought has me leaking profusely.

I reach under my business skirt, lift it, and peel off my powder-blue French-cut panties. Once they're off, I hold them out for inspection.

He takes them, presses them to his nose, and inhales deeply. "You smell extremely wet. Are you, slave?"

"Yes, Master, I am."

"Well, I'll hold on to these… and think about giving them back at the end of your shift. You're dismissed."

I turn, cheeks flushed, and head back to my station. I don't allow myself to breathe until I'm back at my desk. My nerves are frayed. My hands won't stop trembling. It takes me two minutes just to steady my breath. Throughout the day, Lance keeps calling me into his office, just to run his finger through my slit and see how wet I am. Diddling my clit until I'm about to explode… then backing off. Leaving me teetering on the edge of destruction.

Lance studies me like I'm a pet hamster and he's a budding serial killer.

"Do you wish to have your panties back, slave?"

"If it's your will, Master."

"Hmmph. I don't think you deserve them back. As a matter of fact, I don't want you wearing panties to work for the next few days. If I check and you have some on, you will be severely punished. Do you understand?"

"Yes, Master, I understand."

"Good. Now… I want you to make yourself cum." He checks his Presidential Rolex. "You have exactly two minutes. Starting now."

I flip my skirt up, and right there in the middle of my boss's office, I diddle my clit until I jerk, twitch, and skeet cum down my leg, over my heels, and onto the carpet. The orgasm is so intense my knees buckle, my head feels lighter than a helium balloon. I shiver uncontrollably as my nut hits in waves.

"Oh my Jesssuuuss… please, God… I'm cumming ssssoooo haaarrrddd!"

I can't believe the experience I'm having. When the waves finally die down, I ask for permission to go clean myself up.

"Denied," he says flatly.

I'm forced to drive home with dried cum sticking to my thighs. Once I get there, I shower and crash for a quick nap. Four hours later, I wake to my husband walking through the door. I glance at the clock. *10:53 p.m.*

Damn... I was supposed to meet up with Kay. I pray he's not mad at me. That nut I had earlier put me clean out. I'm definitely gonna need more of those.

Harrell sees me naked under the covers and assumes it's all for him. To his credit, even though he's dog tired, he hops into bed and gives me my second nut of the day. Then we both pass out.

AD

"Are you aight, AD?"

"Huh?"

"Are you aight?"

I look up and see Tink standing over me. I must have a scowl on my face or something, 'cause there's concern written all over hers.

"Yeah, yeah... I'm good, T. I just need a drink or something," I tell her.

Truth is, I need more than a drink. It's been a week since I saw the news footage of the shooting at my baby momma Andrea's job. At first, I wasn't too worried, the footage was inconclusive. But earlier today, I called Ten Toes Bonding, and they told me I had a warrant for my arrest. I damn near had a heart attack.

When I heard that news, I knew it only meant one thing, *Andrea snitched on me.*

After all the shit we been through, she ratted me out for that fuck nigga whose dick I caught her sucking in her job's parking lot. I wasn't even going at dude like that. I was keeping it playa, handling my business with my girl. He jumped up on some *Captain-Save-A-Hoe* shit, so I spanked his ass in the lot. Now I got a warrant, and the same bitch who started all this is ratting on me?

I don't wanna do it… but there's no way around it. My baby momma gotta get dealt with. Only question is, *how?*

"Here." Tink hands me a glass of cognac. I'm not a big liquor drinker, but right now I need something to take the edge off before I lose my mind.

I down most of the glass in the first swig, feel the burn crawl through my chest. I kill the rest, hand her the empty glass.

"Make me another one," I tell her.

She takes it, heads to the kitchen.

Tink's a smoker I been knowing since I was a kid. She was my first consistent lick, and over the years we built a bond. Almost like she was an auntie to me. One time I fucked up my pack, and Tink found out. She went out all night—doing God knows what—just to come back and hand me enough bread to re-up. Because of the loyalty and love she's always shown me; I always looked out for her. Any time I needed a place to lay low, she never turned me away.

She comes back with my refill. I gulp that one down too. That warm, fuzzy feeling starts blanketing me, my eyelids getting heavy as my mind drifts.

I start thinking about when I first met Andrea. By the time I realized how freaked out she was, I was already too deep. Then my thoughts slide to my son, AJ. I haven't been a good father—truth be told, there's dudes locked up right now who'd kill for a chance to spend time with their kids, and here I am free… barely seeing mine.

Should I pull up to Andrea's momma's crib? Would she call the laws on me?

There's no telling how long I'll be out here. I need to start building with my son. *Fuck it.*

I open my eyes and catch Tink still staring at me.

"You aight, AD?"

"Yeah, I'm good, T. I think I'm 'bout to go kick it with my son for a lil' bit," I slur, trying to get up off the couch. I didn't realize how hard the drink hit me.

"Boy, you sure you good enough to drive?" she asks.

"Yeah, yeah… I'll be aight."

I pat my pockets for my keys, then think maybe I shouldn't drive my whip.

"T, can I use your car real quick?"

She looks hesitant. If I was sober, she'd have tossed me the keys without a thought. But she must realize I'm too determined to stop, so she digs in her purse and hands me the keys to her Chevy Concord.

"Your ass better bring my shit back in one piece, nigga."

"Thanks, T. I got you, I promise."

I grab my strap, make sure it's fully loaded, and ready before I step out into the world. Tink stays in Pine Creek Apartments. I wouldn't call it the Jets but shit still pops off over here. Since it's right off Federal/Maxey Road, it's technically Crip territory. Even though my squad has a pass all over the city, you still don't wanna get caught lacking, anywhere.

I stuff my strap in my waistband before heading down the stairs and hopping in her car. Soon as I get in, the scent of stale smoke smacks me. Luckily, Tink's one of those rare smokers who actually takes care of herself and keeps her crib and ride clean.

I crank the engine and head toward Andrea's momma's house. When I pull up, I scan for any signs of law enforcement. Even though nobody knows I'm coming, I know how twelve moves, they'll stake out your family and wait for you to pop up. I circle the block once before parking and walking up to the front door.

Andrea's momma lives in the Woodforest North subdivision, a mixed crowd of Blacks, whites, and Hispanics. *Knock, knock, knock.*

A few moments later, I hear her yell, “Who is it?”

“AD!”

There’s a pause, then the locks click before the door swings open. Andrea’s mom, Valinse, stands there looking like a mature version of my baby momma. She’s rocking Daisy Duke shorts and a small yellow tee. No bra, nipples poking. I can feel the cold blast of A/C seeping out the doorway. *The woman’s ’bout to be sixty!*

I know for sure, when she was Andrea’s age, she was a nightmare for niggas. She got her body done five years ago and still goes toe-to-toe with women twenty years younger.

“Hey, Ms. V, I’m tryna see AJ.”

She hits me with that contempt look. Valinse never really liked me. Every time Andrea and I had problems, she automatically assumed it was my fault.

“You didn’t think to call? What if I was gettin’ the starch knocked out my back?”

An image of some nigga bustin’ her down flashes in my head. I don’t know if it’s the liquor or what, but I start looking at Ms. V differently. *I wonder if that pussy still gets wet... or if a nigga gotta use lube to slide in.*

“My bad. I was just passing through the neighborhood and figured I’d stop by.”

I hoped she wouldn’t give me any hassle about seeing my son. I’m not about to tell her I’m on the run and might not have too many more chances to chill with him. I shouldn’t have to. After studying me for a few seconds, she steps aside and lets me in. Her crib feels like a damn meat freezer. *Gotta be fifty degrees in here.*

“He’s in his room,” she says, heading back to her bedroom.

I take a second to appreciate the view from behind, her ass cheeks chewing those denim shorts. I shake my head. *That old ass bitch can get it.*

I walk to my son’s room and knock lightly.

“Come in.”

When I open the door, his face lights up. He tosses the PS5 controller and jumps into my arms.

"Heyyy, Daddy!"

"Wassup, Ju Ju? What you doing?"

"Playing Madden."

"Playing Madden? Boy, what you know 'bout Madden? Who's your team?"

"Eagles," he says proudly.

"Eagles? Let me find out you like Jalen Hurts."

"Of course. East up, Daddy."

I laugh. Something about that convo makes me think of Kay, AJ's godfather. Now that it looks like I might be going in soon, I realize how fucked up it was not making a better effort to hold my nigga down.

"You wanna play?"

"Of course, but you know we not finna play for free," I tell him.

"What you wanna bet?"

"Hmm… how 'bout this, if you win, I'll take you to get snow cones or ice cream, your pick. If I win, you gotta wash the rims on my car."

His little nose scrunches up. He really doesn't like the idea of washing my rims, but he damn sure loves the thought of getting his snow cone or ice cream. Finally, he says, "Bet."

We dab each other up to solidify the deal, then grab our controllers. Of course, he spanks me, and twenty minutes later, I'm standing in line getting him a watermelon-grape snow cone.

On the way back to his grandmother's house, he drops a bomb on me.

"Daddy, why you and Momma don't want me to come home?"

"Say what?" I damn near wreck the car. "How you figure that?"

"Well, I keep asking Granny when can I come live wit' y'all, and she keeps saying, when y'all want me to."

"No, son, it's not like that. Me and your momma do want you home. But them white folks don't want me around, so your momma feels like it's best for you to stay at your granny's until we figure out how to beat them white folks."

He nods like he understands, but I know his young mind can't fully process it. Both of his parents are alive and well, yet he can't live with either one. As a child, I know it don't make sense to him.

I pull up, hand him a hundred-dollar bill. "That's to buy whatever video games you want," I tell him. I know his grandmother spoils him, but I still want him to have his own money.

We park, hop out, and I hug him before dabbing him up again.

"Aight, Ju Ju, I'ma come back soon to kick it with you."

"Facts?"

"Big facts," I confirm with a smile.

He turns, trots up the sidewalk, and disappears into the house. I hate myself for not being there for him more than I have. He deserves to be loved and cared for. As I pull out the apartments, I make a detour to mine and Andrea's spot. Pistol on my lap, I comb the streets of the East, hunting for my rodent of a baby momma.

Chapter 3

Andrea

"Excuse me, I'm new here. Can you tell me what I'm supposed to be doing?" I ask a pretty Hispanic chick walking by.

She stops, turns, and flashes a movie-star smile. Long auburn hair, aqua-green eyes, her beauty is striking.

"Uhmm… well, what department are you in?" she asks.

"To be honest, I don't know. The woman who was supposed to train me really didn't say much."

She starts laughing. "Let me guess, was it Tanya?"

I grin. "Yeah, it was."

"Figures. C'mon, let's go holla at Enrique. He's the shift supervisor—he'll get you squared away."

As she leads me to the back of the hardware store, I can't help but check out her bubble butt. Even though I've dibbled and dabbled with women before, I've never seen one that made me stare. *This woman got my juices flowing.*

I can tell from her demeanor she's from the hood, and I like my women like I like my men, *G'd up from the feet up.*

In the back, a short, stout Hispanic man with thinning black hair and a mustache sits behind a desk.

"Excuse me, E," she says. "We got a newbie, trained by Tanya."

He puts his pen down, shaking his head. "Let me guess, you don't even know where you're assigned to."

"No, I don't," I say with a smile.

"What's your name?"

"Andrea. Andrea Palmer."

He starts typing. "Well, looks like you're in carpentry today. Usually your first two weeks, you'll bounce around departments, so you get a feel for each one. After that, management reviews your work and gives you a permanent zone." I nod, but my mind is still on the other woman. As if reading my thoughts, Enrique says, "Mary, why don't you take her under your wing? I'm sure she could learn a lot from you."

Mary. Now I got a name to go with the pretty face and banging body.

"Sure, why not," she says, extending her hand. "I'm Mary. And from what I've heard, you're Andrea, right?"

"Yup, that's me." I take her hand. "Nice to meet you."

"Nice to meet you too."

Electricity shoots through my body. My pussy starts buzzing. Unless I'm trippin', I swear I feel her fingers graze my palm as we separate. I don't dwell on it, though, I just follow her to the carpentry department. She shows me around; gives me the info I need to get the job done right. I don't know what it is about her, but she got me enchanted.

Our shift flies by. When it's over, neither one of us wants it to end.

"What you got planned after work?" she asks.

"Nothing really. Why?"

"Well, I know this nice lil' Mexican restaurant, if you wanna slide through and kick it. They got the best margaritas in the city," she boasts.

"Sure, I'm down. Just let me run by the crib and freshen up. Give me the address and I'll meet you there."

"Bet."

We exchange numbers, and I head home to wash the day away. While I'm in the shower, I think to myself, *This the first time I ever went on a date with a woman.* I done fucked plenty of 'em, but I ain't never been on an actual date. I honestly don't know what to expect. With men, I know the drill, if their dick's hard, by the end of the night, it's my job to bring it back down. *Simple.* With a woman, I ain't sure how aggressive I'm supposed to be.

I hop out the shower, baby-oil down, and hit myself with a splash of *Nude* by Rihanna. I throw on a black tube dress with some black, four-inch Giuseppe heels. I don't know if I'm overdressed, but I'm damn sure making a good first impression.

I get to the restaurant ten minutes early. Mary's already there, and she looks stunning. She went with a matching skirt-and-blouse set, black with red on the seams. Red pumps, rose-colored Cavalli shades. Now I'm the one feeling *underdressed.*

"Heyy girl, you look fierce as fuck," I tell her. We hug, and I catch a whiff of Elizabeth Taylor drifting off her neck. My mouth waters.

"You clean up nice yourself. I knew you was stacked, but damn!"

The compliment makes me blush, something I wasn't expecting. We sit and order our meals. Since it's her spot, I let her order for me in Spanish.

While we eat, we start sharing pieces of our lives. I tell her about my son and my toxic-ass relationship with my baby daddy. She tells me she just got out of County. She doesn't say why, and I don't ask.

We flirt openly. I catch her looking at me all curious.

"What?" I ask playfully, feeling self-conscious.

"It's just… you remind me of somebody I met in County. An older chick named Charllessa… Charllessa Johnson. You know her?"

I think for a second. "Not off top."

"Oh. I thought maybe y'all might be related."

"Not that I know of."

"Well," she glances at her phone, "it's about 10:45 p.m. This place is about to close. I'm pretty sure you have to be—"

"Nah, I'm good." I cut her off. "I'm a big girl, I don't got no curfew."

"Really?" she challenges.

"Really," I counter.

Thirty minutes later, we're at her crib. My legs cocked open, her face buried between my thighs, her tongue dancing over my clit.

"Ooohhh ssshit… eat that pussy, baby," I moan.

Mary peels my hood back, lightly sucking on the exposed nub. A shiver runs straight through me. I grab the side of her head, holding her in place as she sucks and swipes my clit. My mouth starts watering for her snatch.

"Come put this pussy in my face, baby. I wanna taste that Spanish chocha."

Mary shifts her body, sliding into a sixty-nine. Her fat, juicy pussy hovers over my face. I breathe her in her box soaking wet, juices dripping onto my nose. I bury my tongue in her pussy hole first, then slide the tip between her meaty folds. Finally, I spread her cheeks and go to work.

We're locked in, moving in sync, matching each other's energy stroke for stroke, lick for lick. I feel her shiver in my grip the same time my orgasm starts creeping up hard. I try to hold out, wanting her to cum first… but her tongue game is *ferocious.* I squeeze her ass cheeks, fighting off my own explosion, but still trying to detonate hers. Just as I'm about to blow, she lifts her head and howls.

"Oh fuck! I'm cumming… I'm cummmminnnggg… shit!"

Her pussy skeets and clenches, squirting back into my nose and all over my lips. Before I can even react, my own nut bubbles up and pops. I shove my face between her ass cheeks and growl as my whole body convulses, wave after wave of euphoric pleasure wrecking me.

After that first nut, we lay in bed and talk some more. We agree to take things slow, but both of us curious where this might lead.

Suddenly, Mary gets up and heads to her closet. Seconds later, she comes out with a nine-inch strap-on big, black, and thick as a salami beef roll.

Suffice it to say, the next few hours we spent fucking each other's brains out.

I don't make it back to my apartment until *2:45 a.m.* I walk straight in, fall flat on my bed, and have the most fitful sleep I've had in a long time. *That shower can wait.*

Kelsey

"Make next right." My GPS chirps as I cruise down Woodforest Blvd.

This is the first night I've been out since my boyfriend, Tee Lee, got shot and killed.

Part of me wants to say, *Fuck him.* His slimy ass was supposed to be at home. Instead, he was at my job, in the parking lot, messing with my so-called friend and co-worker doing Lord knows what.

The crazy part? Him and I had just had sex. I know I left his nut sack on E. I don't see why he had to double back and fuck with that backstabbing cunt.

Yeah, I should just say fuck him and leave it alone. But this ain't just about him it's about disloyalty and the repercussions behind it.

I trusted that slut Andrea. Then, instead of being a woman about it, I see her at the police station and the bitch has the nerve to lie to my face *talkin' about her and him were in the car planning to surprise me with an engagement ring.*

I waited for her to come back to work, but the coward never did. Management replaced her, and that's when I found out, *she'd quit.*

Like I said, *coward.*

That's why I'm riding around looking for a spot called *Red's Sports Bar.* Supposedly, it's one of those after-hour joints where hood dudes and bosses come to unwind after the club.

As I make the right, I spot it. The building's not big, but the parking lot is packed. Old schools, candy-coated slabs, and up-to-date foreigns line the rows.

I park my little Nissan Altima and hop out. A gust of wind lifts the hem of my black suede Fendi skirt. I quickly push it down.

Tonight's air has a slight chill, and my nipples harden against the fabric of my cream-colored Fendi top. They'll definitely be noticed when I walk in.

I snatch my matching cream-colored Fendi clutch from the front seat, hit my alarm, and start toward the entrance. I've been messing with Black men all my life, and one thing I know about a hood nigga, he can't resist an All-American white girl. Especially one built like a *Sistah.*

Five-six, 133 pounds, blonde hair, blue eyes it doesn't get more American than me. Even though I'm twenty-three, I like my men older. *Much older.*

The oldest I ever had was a pastor named Dennis Cooper; ironically, also the most dangerous.

Come to find out, he was abducting and killing young women, burying them on church grounds. Say what they want, the man had some good dick for pushing fifty—and he was *very* generous with the coins.

Since then, I've stuck to mostly hood and street dudes.

Tee Lee, Terrance was thirty-six, a D-Boy who sold guns from time to time. Ironically, when he got shot and killed, his dumb ass was unarmed.

All my life, I've gotten hate and flak from Black women claiming I'm trying to steal their men. How is it my fault if a Black man with money would rather deal with a white woman? We're less stress, with more sex. What could be better?

My Valentino heels click-clack against the concrete as I make my way to the front door. The six-foot-four doorman takes one look at me and smiles.

"Baby doll, I've never seen you in here before."

"It's my first time," I admit.

"Really? Well, if you don't find what you're looking for, don't be scared to come find me."

I give him a once-over. He's not really my type in the looks department, but he might be useful to me in other ways.

"I might just do that," I say, honey dripping from my words.

He steps aside and lets me through. Soon as I walk in, the temperature jumps at least fifteen degrees. The place is packed, but it's not wild—just people mixing and mingling.

First thing I notice, there's not many white women in here. And the ones that are can't hold a candle to what I'm bringing to the table.

I head over to the bar, and barely two minutes after I sit down, a brown-skinned, brown-eyed man approaches me.

"How you doing? I hope I'm not bothering you, but I just couldn't help myself. My name's Brazy."

He extends his hand. I catch the glint of his bust-down Patek. Quick appraisal, *definitely a hustler.*

I take his hand. "Hi, I'm Kelsey."

"You mind if I sit with you, Kelsey?"

I gesture to the empty seat beside me. "Be my guest."

I find out he's twenty-five and, evidently, a D-Boy. I ask, "How long you been on the East?"

"Since I was sixteen," he replies.

I find a way to discreetly bring up Andrea's name. He says it sounds familiar, but he's not sure if he knows her. When I mention her baby daddy, AD, he perks up.

"I know *of* him, but he's my big homie and them's age. I know for a fact they know bro."

Based on that alone, I exchange info with Brazy, hoping to get connected to his big homie.

I'm only here for one reason, so I don't mind letting Brazy post up under me the rest of the night. I can already tell, he's the clingy type. Especially if I decide to put this vanilla shake on him.

For someone so young, his convo's decent. I find myself warming up to him, and I can tell he's aiming to get between my milky-smooth thighs. I wouldn't mind letting him take a ride, but I need him fiending for it. The *hope* of a taste will have him wrapped around my finger.

As the spot closes, I let him walk me to my car. Before I slide in, he hugs me tight, gripping the dip in my back. His dick rocks up, pressing into my stomach.

"Damn, Kelsey… you got a nigga on *go* right now. I'm tryna slide to the room with you," he practically begs.

I purr in his ear. "Don't worry, baby… play your cards right, you'll get a taste of it."

He groans as we separate. I hop in my car, pull off, and catch him in my rearview standing in the middle of the parking lot, staring at my taillights like a puppy whining after its owner.

With the first part of my plan in motion, I can't wait for the day I nail Andrea's ass to the tree.

Chapter 4

Kay

I wake up at six-thirty in the morning. Even though I'm back in the *free world*, my body's still trained to wake up at shift change.

I grab my phone and text Hector. He responds immediately, saying he's on his way to scoop me.

Forcing myself to get up, I hit the shower and start locking in my thoughts. Today's my first day back active in the streets.

The plan? Relocate, gain momentum, stack money, build power, then exact my revenge.

True to his word, Hector's been assisting me every way possible. I still got the bread I stacked during our run in the pen, Claudia hadn't spent a dime of it. I'll use that to cop me a whip and a spot to set up shop. I don't know how she paid off my lawyer without my help, but I'll always have respect and love for her because of that.

After I get dressed, I pack some things into a gym bag and head to my momma's room. I knock lightly on her bedroom door.

"Yes," she calls out.

"I'm gone, Momma. I'll call you when I get to where I'm going."

"Aight, baby. I'm going to see your daddy this weekend. You tryna go?"

I think about it. I want to see Pops, but I can't risk it right now.

"Naw, I gotta pass on that. But tell him I love him, and I'll pull up once I get situated."

"Okay, baby. Be careful. Momma loves you."

"Love you too, Momma."

Just as I'm walking away from her door, my phone chimes. Message from Hector: *Cum outside.*

I hoist my bag over my shoulder and step out the door.

The cool morning air is extra crisp. I hop inside his midnight-blue Ram 2500. Soon as I slide in, he greets me with a brotherly hug.

"Kay, mi hermano," he sings out.

"What's good, Hect?"

"Everything, everything."

As we ride, he lays out his plans for me and for the organization we're about to build. While he was gone, a few rival cartel members muscled in on his territory. Naturally, he needs them gone, and I'm the perfect candidate for the job.

"You do this for me, I flood de city for you."

I'll be the first to admit I'm not a killer. My lane is the hustle. But when it comes to survival, I won't hesitate to let my gun bark. A plug of this magnitude? That's survival. So of course, I agree.

No turning back now.

After a forty-five-minute drive down I-10 East, we exit on Garth Road and make a left.

"Where we at?" I ask.

"Highlands. Mi hermano, Nichanor."

I used to pass this exit all the time. I knew it was the East, but we considered it the outskirts never had a reason to come out here.

Eventually, we pull up to a two-story, ranch-style house sitting on a two-acre lot. The neighborhood's quiet. Trucks and SUVs in driveways.

Parked out front is a cocaine-white CLK Benz with vanity plates: *CRTL_B.*

As we hop out, I catch sight of a woman peeking from the upstairs window. I can't make out her features, but her silhouette is dangerous; hourglass shape, wide hips, hair cascading down to her ass.

Hector catches me looking, smacks his lips, and mutters, "Pinche puta." I'm guessing he's not too fond of her.

"Who's that?" I ask.

"Nichanor wife… how you say… sister-in-law?"

I nod, but even after I look away, I still feel her eyes burning into me.

Inside, the scent of something pleasant fills the air. A stout, dark-skinned Hispanic man sits on the couch, smoking a cigar, watching world news in nothing but gray boxer briefs. His neck, wrist, and fingers are dripping gold.

When he spots Hector, he smiles, showing open-face gold plates.

"Hectorio!"

Nichanor stands and gives his younger brother a bear hug.

They separate, and Hector makes the intro. "Dis mi amigo, Kay. He takes care of problem for us."

Nichanor studies me hard. I can tell he's the killer out of the two. *I'll have to watch him.*

After what feels like forever, his scowl turns into a smile. He nods in approval, and we all sit to talk business.

They break down which cartel members I'm supposed to get rid of. I ask if I'm doing this solo.

"Of course not. We give you team," Nichanor says.

"Matter fact…" He pulls out his phone and makes a call.

Not even ten minutes later, two men walk in. I'm thrown off, both look like regular Black niggas from the hood.

"Kay, dis mi sons… Stevie and Jose."

Sons?

Their momma must be Black. I nod in acknowledgment, then turn back to Nichanor so he can explain.

"They're part of our team. Once we take care of those little problems of ours, they'll help build your business up."

From the way he articulates himself, I can tell Nichanor's been in the U.S. longer than his younger brother.

I size up the brothers. "Which one of you is older?"

Stevie raises his hand. About five-eleven, one-eighty-five, taper fade with deep-set waves. Skin tone, double shot of mocha.

His brother, Jose, stands about five-ten, one-seventy-five. Long braids, small scar on his lip. Out of the two, Jose looks like the fighter.

"Well, check game, I'm a younger brother, so I know in these streets, age don't mean much. I look forward to working with both of you fellas."

"Fa sho," Jose replies. His English is crisp, hood inflected. Nichanor must catch my reaction.

"Their mother insisted they grow up here. They head back to Mexico every now and then, "he explains.

Two niggas with blood ties to cartels in Mexico?

I feel eyes burning into me. I look up, and everyone follows my gaze.

Standing at the top of the stairs is one of the baddest women I've ever seen in person. Five-eight, one-forty-five. Long black hair tickling the top of her ass crack, skin tone rich as dark chocolate, honey-brown eyes, body stacked like a brick house. She looks early thirties, but I know she's pushing mid-to-late forties. My mouth damn near drops open.

"Oh, this is the mother of my sons, Tianna," Nichanor announces.

She doesn't even glance my way. Instead, she speaks to Nichanor in Spanish before addressing her sons. I don't catch the words, but I hear Hector smack his lips.

I turn to him. "What's going on?"

"She trip. She no like me."

"Why not?"

"Mi killed her hermano."

My eyes widen. "What! Wait, why'd you do that?"

Hector drops his head, voice heavy with shame. "Thought he was rat… he wasn't."

The remorse in his tone is real. *That's a demon he gonna have to face.*

I think it'll cool down, but Tianna gets heated; yelling, hands flying. Finally, Hector turns to me. "Let's just go, Kay."

He says his goodbyes to his brother, but his nephews trail us outside.

Once we hit the air, Stevie speaks up. "Damn, sorry 'bout that, my nigga. Moms can get crazy. Uncle Petey was her favorite brother."

I turn to Hector. "Why'd you think he was a rat?"

"We had mole inside police station. He say Petey rat. We not know, he fucking Petey wife and want Petey gone. By time we find out, Petey dead."

Damn. That's cold. I'm looking at Hector different now—Petey was family, and he got smoked off the word of a disloyal pig. I shake my head.

"She'll be a'ight," Jose cuts in. "I'm tryna talk 'bout this bidness."

I like him.

"Okay, so what's y'all specialty?" I ask.

Stevie smirks. "Really, a nigga's good at everything, but if I had to pick one—distribution. And accounting."

I look at Jose.

"My thing is marketing going in, clearing out, making room for our product."

I nod, taking it in. "What if I tell y'all I need help with something? Won't take away from our main objective; in fact, it'll push us toward it."

"What you got in mind?" Stevie asks.

Over the next couple days, I run the brothers through my plan.

"We got a cousin who'd be perfect for this. We call him Monstro," Stevie says.

"Okay. When you get the chance, bring him through. Let me get a look at him."

"Bet," they both say in unison before jumping back into their trucks and peeling off.

Hector's whole vibe changes, no longer the happy-go-lucky dude I know. The weight of what he's done is heavy on his shoulders.

"Look, bro, we can wait to go shopping," I tell him. The plan was to grab me a wardrobe and a car to get around in, but now I'm thinking about canceling.

Hector looks offended I'd even suggest it. "Fuck no, bro. We go shop."

"You sure?"

"Of course."

"Okay… where we going first?"

"Where else? The Galleria."

We hop back in his Ram. As we back out of the driveway, I spot Tianna again, glaring down from the bedroom window. I don't know what it is about that woman, but I'm drawn to her. Still, I need to keep myself in check, one thing about these Mexicans, they play for keeps.

As we pull away from the Ochoa house, I remember to ask, "What happened to the police officer who lied on Petey?"

With distaste dripping from his tone, Hector spits, "They find him with throat cut… dick and balls in his mouth."

We ride in silence the rest of the way.

Claudia

It's Saturday, and my nerves are shot. I grab the business card my boss gave me, the address scribbled on the back. I look it up affluent neighborhood.

The clock reads *1:37 p.m.* Since I'm off, I overslept and been lying in bed all morning. Maybe I'm scared to get up, because I know once my feet hit the floor, my day actually starts.

I close my eyes and imagine all the delicious, scandalous things he has planned for me. My chocha starts to salivate.

My hand slides south, middle finger slipping between my folds. The tip comes away wet and greasy. I peel back my hood with my thumb and start flicking my clit.

Biting my lip, I imagine it's Kay who's got me locked into my submissive role. My orgasm starts building. I spread my thighs wide, working my button while my juices bubble, dripping down my ass crack.

Heat spreads through me, my body ready to pop.

BEEP!

The house alarm downstairs. *Someone just walked in.*

I freeze. Harrell's at work. He's not supposed to be home until ten. My ears strain. All I hear is the pounding of my own heartbeat… and dishes clanking in the kitchen.

I throw on a robe, grab my Sig Sauer P226, Harrell bought it for me for when he's gone. I check, fully loaded, ready to shoot.

Creeping toward the stairs, I lean over the banister. No one in the living room, but the kitchen's alive with movement.

Pistol in hand, I slink down the stairs. The noise grows louder. I steady my breath, count to three, and swing the gun around.

"Whoa, whoa! Babe, it's me!" Harrell shouts, dropping a steaming Hot Pocket on the kitchen tile.

All the tension drains from me, like air from a balloon.

"Harrell, what the fuck? Why you ain't say something or call at least?"

"Babe, I did call. You must've had your shit on DND."

He's right. I set my phone on *Do Not Disturb* so I could sleep in.

"What are you doing home?" My tone comes out more accusatory than I mean.

"They gave me the rest of the day off. My supervisor saw how many hours I've logged this cycle and told me to go home," he chuckles.

This ain't good. I wasn't counting on him being home. Now I *gotta* figure out a way to shake him.

He notices my lack of enthusiasm. "Damn, babe. I thought you'd be excited your man can spend some time with you."

"Oh, I am, baby. I'm just a little flustered. I thought you was a burglar… or a would-be rapist."

His eyes drop to the Sig still clutched in my right hand.

"I'd feel sorry for either one of those types of niggas tryna come up in here," he says with a smile.

I glance down at the gun in my hand, then set it on the counter. "My bad, baby."

Harrell takes three steps and wraps me up in a warm, reassuring embrace.

"You good, boo. I should've yelled when I came in, but I thought you might've been sleeping late."

I lean back and look at him. "I was. Matter fact, I just woke up not too long ago."

He wrinkles his nose. "I can tell… you ain't hit your grill yet, have you?"

"Boy, shut up. My breath don't stink like that." I swat at him playfully.

He leans in and gives me a deep, passionate kiss. "I wouldn't care if it did stink, I'd love you regardless."

My heart flutters. Harrell's such a sweet man under that hard exterior. He always knows the right things to say to make a woman feel special. My coochie starts to come alive again, my mouth watering with an uncontrollable craving for some cock.

Without a word, I drop to my knees right there on the kitchen floor. He looks down at me with a knowing smile. He's smart enough not to stop me when I'm fiending for his dick.

I unbuckle his belt, pull his jeans down to his ankles, then slide his boxer briefs out the way. I'm so anxious, I don't even let him take his boots off before my hand's gripping his shaft and my mouth is swallowing his dickhead.

"Mmmhhmm…" I moan around his cock as his precum coats my taste buds.

I work my neck, lips pulling and stretching his rod until he's at his glorious eight and a half inches. I force him deep into my mouth, spearing my face into his lap. He groans, palming the back of my head.

I yearn for Harrell to grab me and fuck my skull with reckless abandonment—abuse my throat until I'm choking and drooling all over his dick and balls. I don't know why I crave being dominated and degraded like that. *Maybe there's something wrong with me.*

I feel him get even harder. I squeeze his balls, trying to hurt myself with the dick. *Ghlup, ghlup, ghlup.*

He shivers in my grip, legs wobbling, knees trembling, before tilting his head back, howling, and unloading in my mouth.

"Agghhh… ssshit… fuccckkk! Damn, babe."

The first spurt slides down my throat with no effort. The second pools on my tongue, and I swallow it quick. The third, lighter, I let sit in my mouth, savoring the salty-sweet flavor of him.

Harrell leans against the counter, catching his breath, while I keep suckling his dickhead, squeezing the last bit of nut from his piss hole.

Once I'm satisfied, I let his dick flop against his leg, grab his boxers, and pull them back up. I shimmy his jeans into place, buckle his belt, then stand and kiss him.

"What did I do to deserve that?" he asks, palming my ass.

"You're a good man. You deserve that… and much more," I tell him honestly. "Matter fact…" I take his hand and lead him upstairs.

If I'm gonna escape suspicion, I need to put this puss on him all day. That way, when I make my move this evening, he won't be asking too many questions.

And that's exactly what I do for the next couple hours.

When *6:30* rolls around, I slide out of bed. Harrell's knocked out—courtesy of the *work* I just put in.

I tiptoe into the bathroom and call my cousin Belinda. Her and I are around the same age. Growing up, she was the one everybody thought was the wild one. She did what she wanted and didn't care what people thought.

Little did they know, *I* was the real buck wild one. I just kept my dirt off my side of town and always used an alias.

If I can count on anybody to cover for me, it's my favorite cousin—Belinda.

Growing up, we've done so much dirt together that if our husbands ever found out, they'd divorce us on the spot.

I text first: *U Busy?*

Two minutes later, she replies: *Sort of. Wassup?*

Claudia: *I need your help. Can I call?*

Belinda: *Hold up. Give me 5.*

I wait it out. Moments later, my phone vibrates and her picture pops up.

"Hello?" I answer in a harsh whisper.

"Girl, why the hell are you whispering?"

"Look, I need you to blow my phone up in about thirty minutes. I'ma tell Harrell Bebe got hurt, and you need me to come over and watch Tito while you run her to the hospital."

"Huh? Bitch, what you got going on that you need to throw my kids under the bus? You know we only use that card when it's serious."

"It is, but I don't have time to explain. I'll tell you everything later, but I need you right now," I press.

She smacks her lips. *"Hoe, I see you still up to your old tricks... but I got you. This better not come back to bite me in the ass. Harrell and I are actually cool."*

"It won't, B. I promise."

"Aight, girl. I got you."

I hang up and hop in the shower. I need to be ready to roll by the time she blows my phone up. Fifteen minutes later,

I'm washed, pulling a shirt, top, and heels from my closet. I toss everything in my bag along with my makeup, throw the bag in the trunk, then head back upstairs.

I take my phone off vibrate, turn the volume all the way up, and place it on the nightstand next to Harrell. Then I lay down and wait.

Sure enough, minutes later, my ringtone blares. I close my eyes and fake sleep. The phone rings through once, then goes to voicemail. Seconds later, it screams again.

Finally, Harrell stirs. "Baby, your phone," he gruffs, clearly annoyed.

"Pass it to me, babe," I say, imitating his tone. He reaches over, grabs it, and hands it to me without even lifting his head.

I answer. "Hello… Huh?… Hold up, Belinda, slow down." I make sure I sound extra concerned. "Okay, okay. I'll be over there. Just calm down."

I jump out of bed, shuffling around the room, grabbing a pair of joggers and pulling them on. After tossing on a thin letterman jacket, I call out to Harrell, "Babe, Belinda's daughter Bebe is hurt. She needs to take her to the ER and wants me to watch little Tito."

"Aight, baby," he mumbles into the pillow, already drifting back to sleep.

I skip down the stairs and jump in my car. "Girl, I owe you one,"I tell Belinda as I crank the engine.

"Yeah, you do. And I want all the tea, don't leave out a drop," she says before hanging up.

I head to a nearby motel, pay for a room for an hour, and spend time getting my makeup right. Once I'm dressed, I text the number on the back of the card. The response comes almost instantly: *8:17. Don't be late or early.*

The clock on my phone reads *7:43*. GPS says it'll take twenty-four minutes to get there. I mash the gas, swerving in and out of traffic like a NASCAR driver.

My heart's racing. Palms sweating.

This is my first time participating in an S&M experience. I figured out my fetish from dealing with aggressive, abusive men in my past. What they thought was disciplining me… was turning me on to no end.

One of my exes, Alex, once made me suck his dick in just my bra and panties while his homeboys sat on the couch watching. As he fucked my throat, he'd call me all kinds of degrading names; slut, trick-ass bitch, his favorites.

I'd be on my hands and knees on the couch, his dick in my mouth, my ass in the air, panties crammed into my crack and soaked through… while his boys ogled my fat-ass cat. Just knowing I was being treated so disrespectfully had my chocha overflowing.

Then there was one of my past flings, Jamichael. Now that boy was a monster. Even though he was younger than me at the time, he fucked me like a maniac. His dick was the biggest I've ever handled. He used that bad boy like a weapon, making me suck him off while choking me with it, wrapping belts around my neck while gutting me from the back.

I could only deal with him in increments. After each session, my body would be completely ravaged… but I experienced some of the greatest orgasms of my life.

Later on, I met Harrell and fell in love. I thought I could put that part of me away, lock it in a closet. But now, that part of me is clawing out of the dark like the boogeyman. And if I don't find an outlet for it, I swear I'll lose my mind.

So, even though I love Harrell, in order to save myself, I have to, no… I *need* to do this.

"Make next left," the GPS instructs.

I turn onto a street lined with nothing but half-million-dollar homes. The house Harrell and I share is nice, but these are on another level.

I park in front of the address and check the time, *8:15*. I sit in the car until my phone reads *8:16*, then step out and walk to the front door. I don't knock. I stand patiently, waiting for the exact moment.

The second my phone reads *8:17*, I ring the doorbell.

Seconds later, my boss, Lance Meyers, answers the door. Dark slacks, white dress shirt with the buttons open, no shoes, and a gold Rolex on his wrist. He glances at the time.

"Very good. Would you like to come in?" he asks, his tone suggestive.

"Yes, Master. May I please come in?"

He smiles and steps aside.

When I walk in, I hear a group of men talking. My heart sinks, but my pussy keeps dripping. Part of me hopes whoever it is will leave soon. Another part, a darker, more sadistic part hopes there are *many* of them. And not only will they stay… but I'll be made to service them all.

Instead of leading me into the living room to greet his guests, Lance takes me into the kitchen. I immediately notice a leash tied to the table; a rhinestone-covered collar clipped to the end. My clit throbs instantly.

"Strip."

That one word almost makes me cum on the spot. I get down to my bra and panties and start to remove them, but he stops me abruptly.

"No. Leave them on… for now."

I freeze in place.

"On your knees."

I sink down. He picks up the collar and straps it around my neck.

"This is where you'll spend the rest of the evening. My associates and I will be visiting you throughout the night. When we do, I expect you to relieve us in any way we choose. Is that clear?"

"Yes, Master."

"Very well."

Just like that, my boss leaves me chained to his dining room table. Nothing on but my bra and panties.

It doesn't take long for the first one to pay me a visit. Surprisingly, it's a Black man. I think I've seen him at the firm, but I'm not sure.

As soon as I see him, I sit at attention on my haunches. He doesn't say a word; just walks up like he's stepping to a urinal. Unzips his fly, pulls out his dick, and grips the back of my head with his right hand. Slowly but firmly, he guides my mouth over the head of his cock.

It's official. No turning back.

I work his dick with fluid precision making sure it's slick and wet, twisting and turning on his shaft. Before long, his body jerks and his cum splashes against the back of my throat. I gulp it down, licking the edges of his head for the extras.

Once he's satisfied, he zips back up and disappears into the living room. Minutes later, I get a new visitor. This time it's a woman. A busty blonde with a short haircut, rocking a charcoal-gray business suit, white pumps, and a set of pearls around her neck. If I had to guess, I'd say she's forty-five… maybe forty-six.

She studies me for a good thirty seconds, like she's trying to decide what to do with me. Then, without a word, she grabs one of the dining room chairs and sets it down three feet in front of me. My guest hikes her skirt up around her waist, pulls her black lace panties down to her ankles. I don't know what she's after, until she bends over and peels her left ass cheek apart with one hand. I take my cue and dive in.

I spread her cheeks wider and lick up and down her crack. The taste of her dirty sweat coats my tongue. I push the tip inside her rosebud, trying my best to tongue her deep.

"Ssshit," she hisses.

Her essence drips from her snatch, the scent heavy in the air. Suddenly she turns, steps out of her panties completely, and sits in the chair bare-assed. She leans back, cocks her legs up, spreading them wide. I crawl forward and feast on her box.

“Yessss… that’s it. You filthy little bitch. Suck on my cunt juice. I ain’t washed it yet, I kept it dirty just for you,” she taunts.

Before long, she bucks and shivers, warm liquid shooting into my mouth. I drink it down greedily, smacking on her sex lips when I’m done. She stands, slips her panties back on, and disappears into the living room. I’m left alone, greasy chin, sodden panties.

The rest of the night is more of the same. I still don’t know how many people were actually in the living room, but I estimate eight men and two women. By 2 a.m., surprisingly, Lance still isn’t one of them.

When he finally comes to release me, he orders me to play with myself until I hit an earth-shattering orgasm, right there on his kitchen floor. My juices puddle on the tile like a house cat that ain’t potty trained.

By the time I get back in my car, I feel drained, like I just ran a marathon. *But I only came once.* My clit feels like it’s still buzzing. After tonight, I know I’ll never be the same.

I stop back at that same motel, shower, and slip back into the clothes I had on when I left the house. I hate deceiving Harrell like this, but until I figure out how to introduce him to this side of me, deception is the only way. Now, I just need to figure out what to do about his brother, Kaydon.

Chapter 5

Rashard

"Okay, check game, Alison you gotta start reading niggas for the money. Some of these clowns be fake flexing, wearing they homeboy's shit or driving they homie's car. To be successful in this game, you gotta decipher through the bullshit."

As we ride, I'm giving Alison the beginner's manual on being a set-up chick. Most niggas who've been robbed don't realize it all started with a female. Sometimes it's as simple as—you fucked her, then ducked her, now she's fucked up about it. Or maybe the nigga doing the robbing is laying that dynamite dick, and she'd set up her own mama to keep getting it. That's why I never let these bitches know exactly what I got going on. *Can't hit what you don't see.*

"Okay, daddy, I got you," she says, eager.

It's been two weeks since the incident at the club, and she's been soaking up game every day. Now, I think she's finally ready for her first run and I know exactly who to sic her on.

Ever since that night she was drunk and I dropped that dick in her, my lil' homie Mexico been begging me to put him on. Course, he don't know I've been slaying her almost every day, sometimes two or three times a day. So fuck it, if he wants a piece of her, it's gonna cost him. Three days ago, I invited the homie over. Him and Alison kicked back, drinking and chopping it up. I told her to make sure she wore something provocative. She slid on red-and-white biker shorts with a tank top, no bra. The shorts were spandex, so her camel toe was on full display. You could see the outline of her lips… even her clit.

After a few rounds, I played sleep on the couch. Fake snores and everything. Not even ten minutes later, I hear Lil Mexico make his move.

"Damn, lil momma, a nigga tryna see wassup wit you. I know you 'bout that action."

"And how you know that?" she fired back with sass.

"Come on now, we not finna play them kid games. We both grown in this bitch. I see how you staring at a nigga."

"Well, I'm not gonna lie, you cute as hell, but a girl ain't tryna just fuck. How I know you not gon' get yours and leave me high and dry?" she countered.

Their conversation dropped into hushed whispers. Lil bro's game was so watered down, I almost fell asleep for real. Alison played hard to get, like I taught her, and after thirty minutes of Mexico spitting his hardest shit, she finally gave him the number.

The last couple nights, they've been going out, but Alison still ain't let him hit.

"I'm not tryna fuck in no dirty-ass trap,"she told him, when he brought her to the same spot he takes all his jump-offs.

Lil Mexico was too cheap to pay for a room, so his plan was to take her out to eat, then bring her back to his crib. Since he thought she was a college *good girl*, he didn't suspect it was a set-up.

As we're riding around the city, I give her some last-minute advice on rocking the young nigga to sleep.

"He's a street nigga, Alison, so you gotta watch what you do and say. The wrong thing will set off warning signs."

"I got you. Just trust me."

"Once you put that pussy on him, fuck him till he can't move. Fix him the drink, and when you know he's out like a light, send me the signal."

I watch her face when I bring up the part about putting the pussy on him. No flinch. No hesitation. *Good.*

We head back to the crib so she can get ready for the evening. On the way, she texts Lil Mexico back and forth, sexual innuendos, subtle promises. Every time he brings me up, she shuts it down.

"He's big bro," she tells him.

Back at the crib, the conversation continues. I lay back on the bed and watch her get dressed. She slips on a red satin thong with the matching bra. I went out and bought her an all-red, backless Pucci dress that stops halfway down her thigh. White, four-inch Bottega heels. There's no way Lil Mexico's gon' think straight tonight. Alison's looking so good, I damn near want to bend her ass over and give her the bidness, but I restrain myself. *Cash first, ass last.*

Once she's ready, she calls him. Twenty minutes later, he pulls up. I make myself scarce and tell her, "If he asks about me, tell him Rah went to some bitch's house on the West." Hopefully that'll kill any thought of me and Alison being a couple.

With her location on my phone, I can monitor her every move. While she wines and dines Lil Mexico, I'm already working on the next mark.

His name, Tiny Tim. Word is, Tiny Tim got big paper and loves to spend it on different women. I've been watching him for the last few days. So far, I ain't seen no cracks in his armor, but one thing I know, everybody has a flaw. All I need is a sliver of space to get through. Once I'm in, it's over.

It's *11:45*. I check my phone; she's heading back to his crib. About six months ago, he bought a two-story in a neighborhood called Summerwood, off the Beltway. To celebrate, he threw a housewarming party. Worst thing you can do? Show jackboys where you lay your head… and that your paper done grown. That same night, I took intel, just in case I needed to take him down later.

Once I see Alison and Mexico have made it back to his crib, I make my way to his neighborhood. A part of me feels bad for corrupting Alison's soul like this. She was truly a good girl. Once this is over, there'll be demons she'll have to contend with.

I turn into the subdivision and park in front of a home with a *For Sale* sign in the yard. I sit back, scrolling through my timeline while I wait. All types of goofy shit going down on the 'Gram, niggas posting jewelry, cars, homes. But the goofiest part? They got license plates and addresses visible. *You'd think niggas would learn by now.*

I make a mental note of all the suckas I'mma try to peel later. Suddenly, my phone vibrates.

Alison: *Chow time.*

I grab my gym bag, my Glock, and make my way to the front door. Hoodie up, face down.

Knock Knock.

The door swings open, Alison's standing there with a self-satisfied grin. I hug her as I step in. Lil Mexico's scent is all over her. I drop the gym bag, unzip it, and hand her a change of clothes, cuffs, zip ties, and a roll of duct tape.

"He's out cold," she assures me. "Drooling all over himself."

Once she's dressed, she slips out of the house, jumps in the car, and drives off waiting on my signal to return.

I grip my Glock G34 GEN 5 with the scope, then head upstairs to the master bedroom. I place my ear to the door, listening. Even through the wood, I hear him snoring like a grizzly bear. I push it open.

Lil Mexico's butt-naked, laying face-down. It's easier to tie his feet first, so that's what I do. He stirs, but doesn't wake. I pull the cuffs, lightly clasp one on his right wrist, then quickly snap the other on his left. Now he's wide awake, only to find himself cuffed, zip tied, and staring at a red beam on his forehead.

"Wh… what the fuck, Rah?" he asks, still foggy from the high-powered cocktail Alison fixed him.

"Yeah, it's me, lil homie."

The gears start turning in his head, he's putting two and two together.

"Damn, dawg, I thought you was my nigga. This how you play the game?"

I can tell he's genuinely hurt. Don't get me wrong, I cut for Lil Mexico—but in this game, ain't no room for friends. Only ones I hold dear are my squad of SHARK niggas. Everyone else? Food.

"Look, dawg, we not 'bout to do all that emotional shit. You know why I'm here, so just make it quick. Come up off it, and I'll be on my way," I tell him.

Of course, he knows I can't let him live, but a part of him *hopes* I will—that maybe our relationship is enough to save him. But he too hard of a lil' nigga to go out like a hoe, so he plays tough.

"Man, fuck you, bitch-ass nigga. I ain't got shit for you—or that nothing-ass bitch you sent my way."

I shake my head in disappointment, though I expected nothing else. Mexico's flaw? He expected a shark not to bite him.

I reach into my bag, pull out a pair of wire cutters. He sees them and starts to tremble. *Nothing good gonna come of this.* Still, he tries to remain steadfast.

I throw on latex gloves, like a surgeon about to perform a difficult procedure.

"To keep it a stack, I fucks with you, lil homie. I really do. But in this world of predator and prey, you gotta be the predator that preys on other predators. That's the only way you stay on top of the food chain. Nothing personal," I assure him. I walk up on him slow, making sure I keep eye contact. He honestly don't know what I'm up to and sometimes, that's the scariest thing. Without warning, I reach out and grab his flaccid dick, pulling until it stretches in my hand.

Before he can react, the wire cutters are pressed against his scrotum.

He starts trembling violently.

"P… please, man, don't do this to me," Lil Mexico stammers, hyperventilating.

Snip!

"AGGGHHHHH!" he howls. I cut a hole into his sack. His right testicle slides out of its protective shield and hangs for the world to see. The smell of fluids fills the room. Screams of pain bellow from deep in his chest, but I don't release my grip.

"Where's the money, nigga? I know you got it stashed somewhere. Just give it to me, and I'll make this shit quick."

Eyes shut tight, he looks like he's about to cry. I don't got time for him to figure shit out on his own. I grip the other side of his scrotum.

"AGGGHHH!"

The wire cutter eats through his sack like paper. His left testicle pops out—now both his nuts hanging outside his scrotum.

"Next one's your dick, dawg. You gon' need that motherfucker," I tell him.

He's shivering, pale, and finally breaks.

"B… ba… bathroom. T… to… toilet."

I snatch the duct tape, cover his mouth, and head for the bathroom.

When I get there, I'm impressed. If you didn't know it was there, you'd never guess he had something stashed behind the toilet. I set my pistol on the counter and start moving the toilet. At first, it won't budge then I notice the bowl isn't connected to the tank.

After closer inspection, I see a small lever on the side of the tank. I pull it, and the tank shifts. A little more work, and I lift the whole thing off its hinges, placing it on the floor.

A hole the size of an NBA basketball is cut into the wall. I stick my hand in, feel around, and pull out bundles of cash wrapped in plastic.

Jackpot.

I knew the lil' nigga had bread, but bundle after bundle, I realize lil' bro was really getting to the bag. All together, it's thirteen stacks. Each stack's gotta be at least ten grand.

I head back to the bedroom, grab a gym bag, and start stuffing it full. Lil Mexico's bleeding bad now, violent tremors shaking his body. I walk up to him, aim my pistol at his head, and say,

"Stay up, lil' homie."

BOCKA!

The hollow point opens his cranium like a pomegranate. I throw the hood back over my head, pull out my phone, and text Alison. By the time I'm walking out the door and down the walkway, she's pulling the dopefiend rental up to the curb. I hop in the backseat, and we take off.

We switch cars, then thirty minutes later, we're back at the crib. The adrenaline got us both geek'd. She's feeling frisky, but all I wanna do is count the money. After her constant attempts to suck my dick, I finally give in. She drops to her knees, her enthusiasm got me bussin' my nut in record time.

After she drinks her fill, we pour the money out on the bed and count it up. *One hundred, forty thousand, three hundred and eighty dollars.* To be real, this is one of the biggest licks I've ever hit by myself. Well… technically not by myself, but Alison don't really get a cut.

We stash the bread, twist a blunt, and pour up some Cognac. Once we lit, we fuck until we pass out. Laying there, watching Alison sleep, I can't help but wonder—

Maybe I done created a monster.

Andrea

As I make the turn onto my momma's street, I can't shake the feeling I'm being watched. I haven't heard from my baby daddy since the shooting. Somehow, the laws got enough to put a warrant out for his arrest. I pray to God he doesn't think it's because of me. I hope he knows regardless of what we go through I would never rat on him. Still, I know my baby daddy. Rationality ain't his strong suit.

I pull up and park in front of my momma's crib. Her car's missing, but that same pickup truck I saw last time is parked in the driveway. Flashbacks of her young nigga bumping into me in the hallway, dick and balls swinging, pop into my head. Something tells me I should just sit in the car and wait until my momma gets back.

Knowing Valinse, she wouldn't leave a nigga in the house alone with her grandson—unless he lives there. So, there's a great chance dude in the house is in there by himself. Being that I *know* my son ain't there, I don't have any legitimate reason to knock on the door. Still, I find myself slinking out of the car and heading to the front door.

Knock. Knock. Knock.

Today, I'm rocking some casual sweats, a PINK hoodie, and a pair of cool gray Retro 11 Jordan's. It's kind of chilly outside, but the wind ain't heavy. I feel my nipples constrict against the fabric.

Seconds after I knock, the door swings open. Standing before me is the six-foot-four young nigga that's been knocking my momma's old walls loose. He smirks, like he can read my thoughts.

"Your momma ain't here. Her and AJ went grocery shopping."

"Oh? Okay… well, I'll just wait."

I don't really wait on his invite. Instead, I make my move, and he steps aside. I walk in and head straight to the kitchen to fix me a stiff shot. I need something to knock off the chill. Two things Valinse keeps in the house—snacks for her grandson, and liquor for her and whoever she's entertaining.

Dude follows but stops in the dining room. I feel his eyes caressing me as I fix a glass of Hennessy and Dr. Pepper.

"You want one?" I ask over my shoulder.

He shrugs. "Sure."

I pour him a stiff one, and we head back into the living room. It doesn't take long before the conversation flows freely. I figure out he's twenty-nine, his name's Dollar, and he's originally from Ohio.

Apparently, he met my mom at a lounge downtown, and they been messing around for about six months. As the liquor warms my body, my tongue loosens up. I boldly ask,

"Do you enjoy fucking my momma?"

Dollar almost spits his drink out. "Huh?"

My face stays stoic. "Do you enjoy fucking my momma? I mean… I know she looks good for her age, but I know her pussy don't get as wet as it used to. So, I'm asking—"

His cheeks flush. "Umm, yeah… I enjoy having sex with your mom. Believe it or not, she gives a lot of women out there ten years younger a run for their money," he claims.

"When was the last time you slid up in a bitch *our* age?" I ask, locking eyes with him.

He looks uncomfortable with my line of questioning. *He probably thinks I'm gonna snitch him out.*

"Don't sweat it. Your secret's safe with me. As long as you ain't beating her ass or bringing her home some type of disease, I could care less who you dropping that heavy dick up in."

I let my eyes roam to his crotch for a second. I spot the obvious bulge, and my pussy instantly starts to moisten.

"Hmmph. It's been a few months," he admits, surprisingly.

"Did she handle that dick like a champ, or did she run from it?"

He clears his throat and subconsciously grabs at his piece to adjust himself. His snake unfurls, and I can clearly see the outline strapped against his thigh. Before he can answer, I prod some more.

"I know it's uncomfortable. Go 'head and let it out the cage."

Dollar groans before sliding his hand inside his shorts, pulling out his thick, long, Hershey-colored cock. I see the relief on his face as his dick finally has room to roam.

I wet my lips. I know I'm wrong as fuck. It's too many men out here in this world to be getting at my momma's piece of dick. But like I said before… *there's something wrong with me.* As Dollar sits on the couch, stroking his cock, I stand. My legs start moving on their own. My eyes stay glued to his dick as I drop to my knees in front of him. I swat his hand out the way, grab ahold of his rod, and lick on the head. His pre-cum tastes citrusy. Without further ado, I open wide and engulf my mom's boyfriend's cock.

"Mhmmm," I moan around him.

"Sssshhiittt," he hisses, tilting his head back. With half his dick lodged in my throat, I yank his shorts down and off. *A bitch needs room to work.*

I spread his legs apart and pull him forward, so his balls hang off the edge of the sofa. My left hand fondles them while my right hand works his shaft steady. "Ghlup, ghlup, ghlup." I bob my head, showing Dollar what a young bitch of my caliber can do.

"Fuck… shit," he groans as I chew his ass up. His right-hand palms the back of my head, forcing me to take him deep. His balls tap against my chin. His dick hardens and twitches.

"Oh shit, oh shit. I'm finna nut. Fuucckkk!"

I jiggle his balls, coaxing out his nut. He bucks, ass lifting off the couch as he unloads globs of thick, sweet cock snot into my waiting mouth. I gulp down the first shot just as the second hits the roof of my mouth. *My mom must be feeding him loads of fruit.*

I gently squeeze on his sack, massaging his balls to pull out the rest of his batch.

"Oooh shit. Damn girl, you a monster," he admits.

I pull back, squeeze his dick until the last drop eases from his slit, lean forward, lick it up, then let it fall.

As I stand, Dollar looks up at me in wonder. My cunt is on fire, and I need to quench it. Just as I'm about to tell him, we hear the garage door opening.

"Shit, Valinse is home," he blurts, scrambling to pull his shorts and boxers up.

I run into the room, grabbing clothes and a wastebasket, trying to look like I'm just here to do laundry. As I walk out, AJ and my mom are coming in from the garage.

"Dollar, that looks like Andrea's car out—"

"Hey, Momma," I cut her off.

AJ hears my voice and lights up. "Momma, Momma!" He takes off in a forty-yard dash.

I set the basket down and scoop him into a bear hug. "Hey Ju Ju, Momma missed you," I sing, kissing his cheek.

My face is inches from his. His little nose wrinkles. "Momma, your breath stinks."

Shame and embarrassment flood me. I scramble for an excuse. "Momma's been drinking a lot of coffee and eating sweets. I haven't brushed yet." He buys it. My mom doesn't. She's giving Dollar that suspicious, slanted-eye look.

She's too much of a vet not to know *something* is off. I pick the basket back up and head toward the garage where the washer is. We lock eyes.

I hope he knows how to play the game, Valinse is no fool. I've seen my mom juggle men right under my daddy's nose. One of them was his good friend, Smitty. I can't say for sure what they were doing, but when I was six, I walked in on them in a compromising position while Daddy was outside BBQ'ing.

After I dump the clothes in the washer, I head back in and straight toward the restroom. As I round the corner, my mom pops up out of nowhere.

"Oh shit," I yelp, startled.

"How long you been here?" she asks, her no-nonsense tone thick with accusation.

I avert my eyes before answering. "Umm, not long."

She sniffs the air, her eyes narrowing. *No doubt, she smells her man's dick on my breath.*

"I'ma tell you like this, you little heffa, next time you see I'm not here, you bet' not set foot in this house while I got a piece of dick runnin' 'round," she growls, menacingly. "You understand?"

"Yes, ma'am."

"Now go wash your motherfuckin' mouth out."

I shuffle past her and head to the restroom. Even though my momma's pushin' sixty, she still puts the fear of God in me when she gets mad. I hit my grill and steady my nerves. I really need to get ahold of myself. One day, I'ma fuck the wrong woman's man and end up in some shit I can't get out of.

Once I pull it together, I head to my son's room. He's on his PS5, playing Madden. Memories of him and his dad playing together pop into my head. I stand there for a few seconds before I call his name.

"Ju Ju."

He glances over, smirks, then grabs the second controller. "You wanna play, Momma?"

Even though I don't know shit about football—except for the fine-ass players I've seen—I sit down and grab the controller. "I'm pickin' the Eagles. Who you want?"

I flip through my mental Rolodex. "What team Odell Beckham play for?"

AJ scrunches his face. "Momma, he don't even play no more."

"Really? Well, what's a good team to play with?"

He thinks a second. "When Dad was here, he played for the Ravens."

My head whips around. "Huh?" My heartbeat quickens. "When was your dad here?"

"Uhhhh… two days ago."

Now I'm trembling. "What did he say?"

I don't know why him seeing AJ scares me so much. I know he'd never hurt our son. I just know AD is a dangerous man. Being on the run for murder, he ain't exactly the most rational decision-maker.

"He said he'll try to come see me again soon. Took me to get a snow cone."

"Oh yeah? What else he say?"

"Nothing really. We just played Madden." He turns back to the screen, ready to start our game.

I go ahead and pick the Ravens. Of course, he beats me 42–3. I didn't stand a chance.

After a few hours together, he finally gets tired. I make sure he's asleep before I sneak out of his room. Closing the door, I head into the kitchen to grab a snack before leaving. That's when I hear noise from my momma's bedroom.

My nosy self can't resist. I tiptoe to her door and lean in.

"If you think I'm playin' with your ass, you got another thing comin'. You gon' sit here and eat this coochie all night," she tells him.

"Yes, ma'am."

Seconds later, *"Yessss, get up in there. I want the tip of that tongue ticklin' my uterus."*

I shake my head and walk off. *Momma's a stone-cold freak. That's where I get this shit from.*

I grab the keys off the coffee table, lock the door, and head to my car. It was cool earlier, but now it's cold as hell. I run and hop inside, crank the heater up.

I think about what my son just told me; AD was at my momma's just two days ago. *What if he would've been here when I pulled up? How would he have reacted?*

I've tried to reach him, but his phone always goes straight to voicemail. Knowing him, he probably tossed it. Something in me says I need to get to him before he gets to me—otherwise, it might be disastrous for our family.

Chapter 6

Demon

"Damon, my boyfriend's comin' to spend the weekend over here. I know you don't like bein' here when he does, so…" my sister Debra says, as I'm loungin' on the couch watching *Power*.

"Psssht." I smack my lips. Truth is, I'm not feelin' dude… or any other dude for that matter. I know he's stickin' dick to my sister, and I'm not tryna sit here listenin' to her get her back beat in.

"Yeah, a'ight. What time he pullin' up?"

"Around nine tonight."

I glance at my watch, it's a little after seven. "I'ma make a move then."

"Damon, you know you don't have to leave. You pay bills here. Sometimes you pay all the bills. I don't want you to feel—"

"Naw, sis, I understand. You grown. You gon' have boyfriends and all that ole shit, but I'm not 'bout to be up in here listenin' to y'all fuckin'. I ain't with all that," I tell her.

She sighs, giving up. We've had this conversation more than a few times. I know what the deal is, but I'm not goin' for it. She keeps cooking while I pull my phone out. My uncle's out of town, so I can slide through there.

I scroll through my contacts. First name I see, AD. Brodie's on the run, so that's out. Next is Rah. Definitely not. *Fam's too snaked out for me.* I scroll back up and land on Keeda's number. I dial.

"Hello?"

"What's good, you busy?"

"Actually, I'm not. Why, wassup?"

"You got somethin' goin' on tonight?"

"Naw, not really. Why, you tryna do somethin'?"

"Check game, I'm 'bout to leave the crib. I'ma pull up on you and we can check our schedule."

"Okay, well I'll be waitin'."

"Fa' sho."

I get up and get my shit together. Pack a few changes of clothes in a gym bag, snatch up my new Mossberg MC2SC pistol and my Kel-Tec RDB, then place them in the trunk of the car me and my sister share. Really, it's my car, but since she's in college, I let her use it most of the time. Being that her boyfriend will be over all weekend, she can use his whip to get back and forth.

I head back inside and wait for her to finish cooking. After we eat, I make my way to Keeda's spot. She stays on the Southwest side of Houston, off a block called Club Creek. Even though I've touched all four corners of the city, I don't really fuck with cats from the Southwest. Especially spots like Club Creek.

As I turn down her street, I set my Mossberg on my lap. My brand-new bitch, picked up from a gun shop owner who liked to smoke crack on his downtime. Hopefully, I won't have to use it while I'm out here.

I make a left into her apartments and immediately spot all types of niggas outside—most of 'em draped in blue. I don't know if they *rep* or they *trip* out here, but I park and hit Keeda on text. She sends her apartment number and tells me to *come in*.

Walking away from my whip, I hear hushed whispers. Even though I'm not flaggin', I'm still draped in Blood. *Us Sharks don't flag or brag, we body bag.* I know they ain't feelin' some out-of-bounds ass nigga steppin' on their turf, in opposition colors, comin' to fuck one of their bitches.

I keep the strap tucked and concealed as I knock. *Knock. Knock. Knock.* I can feel the stares at my back, but I pay 'em no mind. Seconds later, Keeda answers the door, black silk robe loosely tied at the waist, washboard stomach on display, smooth toned thighs glistening with cocoa butter.

"Boy, you ain't waste no time gettin' out here. Most niggas say they on their way, but don't pull up for at least two hours."

"Well, I'm not most niggas. If I tell you I'ma do somethin', it gets done when I say, how I say," I reply with conviction.

She smirks, steps aside, and lets me in.

Keeda and I been fuckin' around for a couple months now, but this the first time I've been to her crib. When we link, we always get a room. No way I'm bringin' her back to the spot where my sister lays her head.

As I walk through, I take in her setup. She told me back when she and Kay were fuckin' around, she ain't have a job, did hair to get by. Now she's workin' at the post office, pullin' $28 an hour. Crib's fully furnished, and she dropped cash on a brand-new car.

I watch her ass move under that silk robe until she stops, turns, and asks, "Would you like somethin' to drink?"

"Sure. What you got?"

"Everything's in the kitchen cabinet, help yourself," she says over her shoulder as she heads to the back bedroom.

I walk into the kitchen to see what she's workin' with. After fixing me a Ciroc and Sprite, I stroll around her living room, being nosy, looking for pictures.

Knock. Knock. Knock.

Somebody's at the door. My first thought—let 'em keep knockin'. This ain't my crib. But they keep at it, so I go ahead and answer. Soon as I do, I regret it.

Standing there is a five-eleven, dark-skinned nigga with dreads. Draped in royal blue. Even the rubber bands in his dreads are blue. He tries to look past me into the apartment.

"What's craccin', Cuz?"

I flinch, grit my teeth, and let him know respectfully, "Ain't no Cuz over here, my nigga. This Blood bidness."

He smirks, confirmation of what he suspected.

"Where Keeda at? I'm tryna holla at her."

"She in the restroom right now," I tell him. He inches closer like that's gon' make me move. Instead, I stay planted. "I'll let her know you came by. What they call you?"

He don't like it. With disdain, he spits, "Tell her Kenny Cuz came by."

"Yeah, a'ight. I got you." I step back and close the door in his face. *Fuck that nigga.*

I'm salty at the disrespect, but I don't let it get to me. I keep sippin', waiting for Keeda to finish washing her ass. When she finally comes out, she looks amazing—cream-colored Hermès wraparound dress, off-white Fendi heels to match. I catch her fragrance but can't name it. I just know it wasn't cheap.

"You ready?" she asks.

"Yeah, but where we goin'?"

"It's a surprise. I'ma drive."

I follow her lead, and we step out. Soon as we hit the stairs, I spot Kenny and a few of his homies huddled at the bottom. The air's thick with animosity. It don't help that Keeda's killin' it, lookin' like a Hollywood actress.

I think Kenny's about to make a scene, but surprisingly, he doesn't. Guess he don't wanna look like a sucka in front of his boys. As soon as we slide into her car, I turn to her.

"What's the story with you and that nigga Kenny?"

She looks caught off guard, no reason to think I know who Kenny is. This moment's gon' define our situation. If she lies and I find out, trust is dead. If she keeps it a buck, I'll ride for her.

"We used to mess around a while back. Had to let him go. His ass was too controlling. Plus, he was always tryna confiscate the lil' coins I was gettin'. Talkin' 'bout, let him flip it and he'd double my money. When it came time to pay me back, he always had a sad story." She spits the last part with venom.

I study her for signs of deception. She seems solid, so I lace her up. "He came by earlier lookin' for you. I guess he expected me to let him in, but that ain't happenin', especially if I ain't talked to you about it first."

I see a tight smile. *She likes that I didn't fold under pressure. Never that.*

"I don't know why he wanted to come in. He knows ain't shit poppin' wit' us. Him and I haven't linked up in almost two months."

I hear her, but I've learned, when it comes to women reppin' their body counts, believe half of what you hear.

"Well, fuck all that. I ain't tryna talk about no other nigga. Where you 'bout to take me?"

She smiles. "You ever been to the Aquarium?"

"Naw."

"Well, that's where we're goin'. I hope you like seafood."

"I love it," I tell her. We talk shit the rest of the way there.

Dinner was cool. I really enjoyed myself. On the way back, I'm tryna figure out how to slide in the idea of spending the weekend with her, but Keeda beats me to it.

"So, wassup? You wanna waste money on a room, or you wanna come spend the night at my crib?"

"Shit, fuck the night. I'm tryna kick it with you for the whole weekend."

She can't hide her smile. "I'm cool with that. You need to run to the house and get some clothes?"

"Naw, I'm good. I always keep three or four sets in my trunk at all times. You never know when you might need to make a quick exit."

She can smell the bullshit but doesn't call me out.

We get back to her crib around eleven-something that night. I'm on high alert. No doubt, her lil' ex-boyfriend Kenny gon' be extra salty when he hears I'm at her spot all weekend. I'm not the type to beef with a nigga behind a broad, but I will spank a nigga off principle. Luckily, nobody's out when we pull up.

As soon as we step through the door, Keeda's all over me. Before I even process what's goin' on, she's on her knees and my dick is down her throat. *Ghlup. Ghlup. Ghlup.*

With my back against the front door, shirt tucked under my chin, pants around my ankles, I palm the back of her head as she chews me up like a piece of beef jerky. *Damn... she's a fool on the dick.* I see why Kay used to run out here all hours of the night just to get a taste of this.

I feel my balls tighten; she does too. Instead of finishing me off, she lets my cock fall from her mouth. "I want the first one in my ass,"she tells me. My dick twitches, and I damn near skeet on the spot.

Keeda grabs my hand and leads me to the bedroom. Twenty minutes later, I'm shooting my first load into her ass, filling her to the brim. After licking me clean, she gets me back up, and I fuck her into the mattress. We don't stop until the sun comes up.

As she sleeps on my chest, snoring, I eye the bedroom door. I know bein' over here with Keeda is 'bout to bring a world of problems. *I hope this bitch is worth it.*

Kay

Sitting in the driver's seat of the brand-new Tahoe I just snatched, I get ready to make the call I've been procrastinating on. I know once I set things in motion, I won't be able to stop the avalanche.

I log on to our website, find the code number, then hit the TextNow app. The phone rings, and someone picks up. *"Eat,"* he says.

"Or be ate," I respond.

"Who dis?"

"This Kay. What's good, Shark?"

It's been a minute since I've spoken to King Mako. He's been on the move, out of town the whole time I've been gone. Word is, he's been expanding the organization. I've been down with the Sharks since I was sixteen. Mako's big brother started it, but some say their cousin put the bread behind it, a pimp nigga named Saint Lucian.

Once I got down, I put the whole click on. Even though me and my niggas are Bloods, the Sharks come first. Only the most elite hustlers and killers get in.

Part of our oath was to always have our *Brodie's* back. When I took the charge for Rah and them, by the law of the game, they were supposed to handle their responsibilities. But before I made my move on them, I needed clearance.

"You know me, I'm always on the move. I'm in Ohio right now, layin' the foundation," Mako says.

"Overstood. Well, the reason I'm callin', I don't know if you knew, but I got forty years for two aggravated robberies. To keep it all the way Hot, it was Brodie Rah and them's lick. I kept my mouth shut, took the charge, but them niggas left me stuck."

"What? What you mean, they ain't get you a lawyer, bond, commissary—nothin'?"

"Brodie, they ain't get a nigga shit. I ain't heard from them in over two years."

"Damn. What district y'all in?"

"District 015."

Mako gets quiet. *"I'm assuming you want clearance."*

"Yeah, I do," I reply.

"On what level?"

"Full payment. I was hearin' a little about your situation through the pipeline. Didn't know it was that serious though."

I can almost hear the gears turning in his head as he weighs the decision. Finally, he gives me what I want.

"Clearance granted."

I'm elated he gave me the green light. Truth be told, I was gonna get at them niggas regardless, but now I don't have to worry about repercussions from the Brodies.

When we hang up, I call a nigga I used to go to church with as a little boy; Ricky, or Rick for short. He's a private investigator now.

"Hello?"

"Where you at?" I ask, eyes on my rearview.

"My GPS says I'm two minutes away. This shits like the country out here," he comments.

With Hector's help, I copped a crib down the street from his family. I ignore Rick's comment, hang up, and wait for him to pull up.

When he does, he's driving a black Ford Taurus SHO. I watch him hop out, brown attaché case in hand, and head to the passenger side of my truck.

I unlock the doors. "Wassup, boy?" he greets as he slides in.

"What's good, Rick? What you got for me?"

He pops open his case, pulls out a manila folder, flips through it until he finds what he's lookin' for. Then he starts breaking down all the info he's gathered.

It's astonishing what a couple grand can accomplish. We spend the next thirty minutes going over each item in his file. I pay him and hand over his new assignment. He hops out, and just like that, the ball's officially rolling.

Two Days Later

"So look, Kay, Pancho and his son PJ are at this lil' cantina called Chulo's. They heavy up there, but once they leave, we'll be able to get the drop on 'em,"Stevie laces me up as he drives, me riding shotty.

Jose's in the backseat of the Tahoe, Kel-Tec P50 laying across his lap. Fresh fifty-round clip in it, with another in his cargo shorts pocket.

"So, what's the move?" I ask, thumbing my Walther Q4TAC.

"Both them niggas married, so they can't take the lil' bitches they scoop back to the crib. We'll lay back and follow 'em to their duck-off spot. We got a chick inside right now, keepin' tabs on 'em. Soon as they leave Chulo's, she's gonna come out and jump in the truck with us. We'll use her to try and get inside the spot."

"Okay… so when we go in the crib, what's the objective?"

Jose chuckles behind me. "Kill everyone, bruh, what else?"

That's what I figured. Don't get me wrong, even though I agreed to this mission, I'll be the first to admit, I'm not a killer. My whole life, I've been taught dollars and dead niggas don't mix. As long as a nigga don't get in the way of my paper, there's no reason to resort to violence. But in this case, I gotta go *through* these niggas to get to my paper. *So be it.*

We pull up to Chulo's and park across the street, next to a building. From here, we can see everybody coming and going. Twenty minutes in, Stevie gets a text.

"Pancho and PJ are about to leave," he says aloud.

I straighten up, my heart kicking harder. A part of me wishes something would happen to make us call it off. *Wishful thinking.* Nothing short of God Himself is gonna stop the Reaper from claiming Pancho and his son.

Ten minutes later, we spot Pancho, PJ, and two young women stumbling out of Chulo's. By the looks of it, the two men are drunk as hell. Still, we don't underestimate them, or the situation. No matter how lit they seem, they're both seasoned killers and still a dangerous threat.

Pancho's driver pulls up to the curb, and all four of them pile into a blood-red Ford Excursion.

"Where's your girl at, and how we supposed to keep a tail on 'em if we gotta wait on her?"

Stevie smirks. "You'll see."

Seconds after the group disappears, we pull up to the front door of the club. A petite Mexican chick with wavy hair and light blue eyes comes speed-walking out, phone in hand, and hops in the truck next to Jose.

"Wassup, Yana," Stevie greets her.

"They're on I-10 going east," she announces.

We fall back, keeping distance so they won't suspect they're being tailed. Then a thought hits me, *Jose said we were about to kill everybody. Does that include Yana?* Watching her eagerness to help, I can't help but feel a little fucked up about what might happen to her.

"Turn right here."

Stevie makes a left into a residential street in a neighborhood called Songwood. We're just in time to see the group get dropped off, the driver pulling away to leave them their privacy for the night. Once they disappear into the house, we get ready.

This is it. The point of no return.

The plan is for Yana to walk up to the door and ring the bell. Once one of the two men glances through the peephole and sees a young, barely dressed woman standing there alone, they won't hesitate to open up.

Stevie and I will be crouched on the side of the door, out of sight. As soon as it opens, we'll push through, sticks up, hot and ready. Jose will cover the back door in case somebody tries to leave the party early.

We jog down the street, make a U-turn, and approach the house from the neighbor's yard. Once we're in position, Yana will walk across the street and head straight for the front porch.

We're set.

Ding... Dong.

She rings the bell and waits. A male voice approaches, laughter filling the foyer.

"Who is it?"

"Yana."

"Yana?" He sounds surprised.

As the locks click open, I steady my breathing. Subconsciously, I glance at Stevie—he's calm, like the eye of a storm. Like he's on a stroll in the park.

Suddenly, the door swings wide. Light floods the porch.

"Yana, ¿qué pasó?"

Before she can answer, we move. I grab Pancho by the neck, shove him back, and send him stumbling. He hits the floor hard.

"Oooff!"

I don't give him the chance to scream. I jam the barrel into his eye socket and squeeze. *BOCKA.*

A sick thud follows as his skull bounces off the ground and splits open like a watermelon. Blood splatters my face. Something greasy catches between my teeth. I don't spit, just wipe my mouth and see bits of bone and hair stuck there. I smear them off on my shirt.

I catch Stevie rounding the corner, muzzle flashes lighting the hallway. *BOCKA... BOCKA.*

I jump up and rush to him. In the living room, I spot the two women from the club, half-naked, titties out, dead on the sofa.

Fuck... where's AJ?

Like he read my mind, Stevie motions for me to check the back.

I raise my tool and edge toward the hallway, moving fast but cautious. Doors line both sides. First one on the right is closed. I twist the knob, push it open, nothing.

Just in case it's a setup, I keep the strap up and ready. I take two steps in, then hear a door behind me swing open.

I turn and see the barrel of a gun.

Instinct kicks in. I dive right just as fire erupts. *BOCKA! BOCKA! BOCKA!* Heat sears past my ear. Sheetrock explodes, slugs punching lemon-sized holes through the wall.

I scramble to get out of the kill zone. *BOCKA! BOCKA!*

Two more shots, but they're not from PJ. I look up and see Stevie chasing somebody down the hall. I push up, take off after them.

The back door's wide open, PJ's outside. Stevie's just crossing the threshold when—

Pap! Pap! Pap!

A three-round burst shreds the night air. As I rush through the doorway, Jose's standing over PJ's lifeless body, Kel-Tec still smoking. Half of PJ's head is crushed, a thin exit wound dead center in his back.

"We gotta go," Stevie reminds us.

The four of us rush back to the Tahoe where Yana's waiting. We don't even make it out of the neighborhood before sirens start wailing in the distance. Sweat beads roll down my forehead. My hands still tremble from the adrenaline. *I almost got my head blown off,* is all I can think.

Jose pops the trunk, snatches a gym bag, and stuffs his straps inside.

Twenty minutes later, Stevie drops Jose and me off at their mom and dad's crib. I ask where he's headed.

"To take Yana home."

The way he says it, I know she'll be dead before sunrise. I glance at her, she's playing on her phone like she ain't got a care in the world. *She must have complete trust in the brothers.*

Once Stevie pulls off, Jose and I step inside. I haven't been here since the time I came over with Hector. Their pops seemed cool enough, but the verdict's still out with their T-Lady.

Most of the lights are off. The living room TV's dark. Either they're upstairs asleep, or nobody's home.

"You want somethin' to drink?" Jose asks, eyeing my hands. That's when I notice they're still trembling slightly.

"Sure. What you got?"

"Shit, what don't they got? Between Moms and Pops, they drink everything. Clear or brown?"

I think for a second. "Brown," I say, sinking into the plush sofa. My eyes wander, taking in the pictures scattered around the living room. One in particular catches my attention, it's their mother, Tianna, with who I assume is her brother, Petey.

That's fucked up he died a traitor's death, especially being innocent.

"Here."

I take the glass from Jose and sip. "Is that Petey?" I nod toward the photo.

He glances over. "Yeah. That's my Uncle Petey, Momma's baby brother. When he came to the States, he stayed with Moms. She feels responsible for his death because she introduced him to Pops and his side of the family. Even though she didn't want him involved, you couldn't tell Unc nothin'. Most of Mom's side of the family understands why Uncle Hect did what he did, but some ain't tryna hear that shit."

"Shit, to keep it G, I don't know if I'd hear it either. To know my family died behind a dirty-ass pig?" I shake my head in disgust.

"I know. Uncle Hect tried to make it right by spanking the pig, but…"

We both know, it was a respectable gesture, but pointless. *Nothing could bring Petey back.*

I finish the glass, and Jose makes me another. My bladder starts barking.

"Damn, where y'all restroom at?"

"You can use the one upstairs. Downstairs toilet be trippin' sometimes."

"Which one's the bathroom? I don't wanna walk into the wrong room and have your pops blow my wig back," I joke, only halfway.

"Nah, you good. Pops out of town. When you go upstairs, it's the third door on your left."

I knock back the rest of my drink, then push myself up and head for the stairs. *Damn... did he say third door on the left or right?* I'm too lit to remember.

Fuck it, I go right.

As I approach the third door, I hear R&B music playing. Logically, I know this ain't the bathroom, but I twist the knob anyway, pushing it just enough to see through the crack.

What I see freezes me in place.

Tianna's on the bed, naked. Even with the lights off, the moonlight cuts through, making her juices glisten as she works a solid black dildo, thick as my wrist, into her pussy. Her lips are thick and plump, gripping that rubber shaft as it plunges in and out of her sopping wet cunt. Even from this distance, I can see the white froth building on the fake dick.

Squelch. Squelch. Squelch.

My dick starts to ache. Her legs are spread wide, my mouth watering. I'm tempted to pull my shit out right there in the hallway. Hard as it is, I tear myself away and rush to find the bathroom.

As soon as I shut the door, I whip it out and get to work. Not even two minutes later, I'm busting all in the sink.

"Fuuuccckkkk," I groan in ecstasy. *Damn... she got a fat-ass pussy.* Fat like Claudia's.

Once my piece deflates, I take a much-needed piss, then wash my hands and head back downstairs. Jose's on the couch, caking with some female. You'd never think he'd been part of a quadruple homicide just a few hours ago. I can't stop thinking about Tianna and what I caught her doing.

I pull out my phone and scroll through my contacts, but it's late as hell, so nobody picks up.

"Say, bro, I'm 'bout to bounce. I'll catch up with you niggas later," I tell him, standing up and making my way to the door.

Jose daps me up, and I step outside.

As I hop in my truck, something tells me to look up, and there she is. Tianna. Staring out the window at me. I can't tell if she's wearing a robe or still butt-ass naked. I stand there, hypnotized. There's something about this woman that pulls me in. I haven't spoken a single word to her, but I feel like we're connected.

Finally, I break eye contact, fire up the truck, and pull off. Tianna stays on my mind the whole ride home.

The next day, Stevie, Jose, and me link at my crib. I don't ask Stevie what happened when he dropped Yana off, based on the energy he's giving, I already know.

"We just got word, Chucho's in Mexico right now. He won't be back for a few months at least. Pops said we can go ahead and build on the business now, and when Chucho pulls back up, we'll pull up on him,"Stevie says.

We're sitting around drinking Cognac and watching *SportsCenter*.

Jose sets his gun down and turns toward me. "So, what was it you wanted to talk about?"

I'd texted the brothers early this morning telling them I had something to run by them. At first, I figured I'd have to wait until we handled the problem, but with Chucho out of town, *now* is as good a time as any.

I spend the next hour laying everything out. They're hesitant at first, but once I show them how lucrative the plan could be, they're in.

"I think we'll need to bring one more nigga in on this, "Jose points out.

"I think you're right. Who y'all got in mind?"

The brothers glance at each other and smirk. "Monster," they say in unison.

"Who's Monster?" I ask, intrigued.

"Trust us, he's somebody you want on your team. And he's family. Our cousin on Momma's side."

"Okay, it's settled. Get at Monster and let him know what the play is. Let's all meet up tonight and start putting everything together."

After dapping the brothers up, I watch them head out. Now that I've got my new team in place, it's time to start building my empire, *brick by fuckin' brick.*

Chapter 7

AD

Two Weeks Later

It's almost six in the evening, and I'm parked outside the apartment Andrea, and I used to share. It's been three hours since I pulled up, and still no sign of her.

One of Tink's homegirls, Sharday, popped up at Tink's earlier. I had her slide to Andrea's job to see if she was still working there. Come to find out, Andrea quit right after the shooting. The next logical move is to stake out her spot. I have to be careful though, the laws are lookin' for me, and her apartment is the first place they'd check.

So here I am, ducked down in Tink's car, watching and waiting for her to show her face.

I pull a Newport short out the box and light it. I've never been a big cigarette smoker, but ever since I smoked that nigga at Andrea's job, I've been runnin' through damn near a pack a day.

As I pull on the cancer stick, I spot a familiar face walking through the breezeway. Light pink sundress, hair up in a bun; Cassi's lookin' good as ever. I wanna hop out and pull up bad. Just seeing her makes me realize I haven't gotten my dick wet in almost a month.

But being on the run, a nigga can't afford to link with the wrong bitch. For some, that $5,000 Crime Stoppers tip is too much to turn down. Not saying Cassi would snitch, but I can't take the risk.

I watch discreetly as she walks to her car, hits the alarm, and slides into the driver's seat. Her juicy bubble wobbles under the thin material of her dress. *Yeah... I definitely need to get some pussy soon.* But who?

After Cassi drives off, I crank the car and head back to Tink's. It doesn't take long to get there. When I park, I notice Sharday's car is still outside.

Sharday's one of Tink's longtime smoker friends. She's the type to smoke but still handle her business so well, you'd barely know she's on it. About 5'5", a buck thirty-five, skin like Dutch chocolate, with a nice bubble butt. If she wasn't a dopefiend, she might've had a shot at being on a nigga's roster. At forty-three, I know she was one of the baddest women around back in the day.

I park and head inside. Soon as I walk in, I can tell they just finished blowing a bolo. The air's thick with that pungent smoke. Both women are on the couch, glassy-eyed. Tink's fidgeting with her bracelet, while Sharday can't stop opening and closing her thighs—no doubt giving her coochie room to breathe.

Tink sees me and smiles. "Heyyy, AD," she sings, clearly zooted.

"Wassup, what y'all got goin'?" I ask, dropping onto the sofa next to Sharday. She closes her eyes, bites her lip, letting the high take her wherever she needs to go. I keep the conversation light, they clearly want to enjoy their high, but I can't help noticing Sharday rubbing her pussy through her shorts.

My dick twitches. Thoughts of bending her dopefiend ass over start flooding my mind. Her eyes stay shut, her body trembling lightly. She balls her fist as the crotch of her shorts darkens. If I didn't know better, I'd swear she just tinkled on herself.

Did she just cum?

The thought alone's got me bricked up. *I'm trippin'.* I stand, tent obvious in my pants, and make for the restroom.

I splash cold water on my face, trying to collect myself. *She's a whole dopefiend. But damn, she still looks good. I bet she got some A-1 ... I can tell her cat gets super wet.*

"Come on, dawg, get yourself together," I mutter, over and over.

Once I've got my dick under control, I head back to the living room. This time, Sharday's sitting alone. Her high's come down some—but not all the way.

"Where's Tink?"

"Out gettin' some money," she replies.

Tink once told me when she's really zooted, she likes to go out and get a bag—*by any means*, she'd always say.

"I'm surprised you didn't wanna stretch *your* legs," I tell her, sitting in the recliner.

Sharday leans her head back, eyes closed. "Naw. When I get high, my mind's on somethin' else."

I can tell.

"Like what?"

At first, I think she doesn't hear me. But after a few moments, she leans forward, opens her eyes, and says

"Dick."

My eyebrows furrow. "Dick?" I ask, intrigued.

"Yeah, dick. When I get high, my pussy gets unbelievably wet. Sometimes, I'll even nut on myself."

I can't help glancing at her crotch. Looks like she pissed on herself. *Damn... her shit IS saturated.* She catches me looking.

"You don't mind if I hit another one, do you?"

"Shit, do you."

She pulls out her tools, stuffing a fat-ass dime rock into the end of her straight shooter. Before she hits it, she pauses.

"Oh, my bad, where are my manners. You wanna hit it?"

My face twists up instantly. I'm half a second from cussing her ass out, but instead, I bite my tongue and decline. "Naw, I'm good. I don't smoke."

"I figured you didn't, but I still had to offer." She thinks for a second. "Do you sniff?"

Truth is, coke ain't my drug of choice, but I have snorted a couple times—usually when I'm with a bitch I'm tryna fuck. Lil' liquor, a couple lines, and I'll beat a bitch's back in for hours.

"Every now and then," I admit.

Sharday sets the pipe down and rummages through her purse. Doesn't take long before she finds what she's after. She tosses a small baggie of white powder onto the coffee table.

"Do you, baby."

I shrug, dump about a gram of coke on the back of my phone, roll a dollar bill into a tube, and snort two fat lines. My whole body goes numb instantly.

While I'm floating, Sharday puts fire to the end of the straight shooter. After two good hits, her eyes glaze over. I watch as she slips into a euphoric transformation—first the trembles, then she closes her eyes, balls her fists, and nuts on herself again.

When her orgasm fades, she opens her eyes and stares at me like a wolf sizing up a sheep. "I want some dick."

It sounds more like a demand than a request. I don't say a word. Just reach for my belt buckle. I barely get it undone before she's on her knees, stuffing me into her mouth.

My first thought, *damn, I hope I'm not too high.* I've heard sometimes your shit won't work if you're too lit. But the second her warm lips wrap around my cock; all my worries vanish. Within seconds, she's got every inch of me hard as a brick. Her mouth's hot, wet, damn near perfect.

"Hold up, hold up," I tell her. She backs up.

I strip down to my black Jordan socks, then sink back into the couch, bare-assed. Sharday follows my lead, peeling off her shorts, then her panties.

I sit there in awe. The inside of her drawers is lathered with creamy white nut. Her pussy's hairy, but not wild or nappy like I expected, neatly trimmed, pubic hairs slick and laid down.

Instead of going back to sucking me off, she pushes me back and climbs on my lap. I'm thinking, *damn, I don't have a rubber.* She's a smoker, and ain't no telling what she does with her pussy.

Before I can protest, Sharday reaches back, grabs my dick, and slides down on it.

"Fuucckkk… sssshit," she groans as I fill her up. Her pussy's hot as an oven, juices already running down my balls.

"Mmmhm… boy, you got a big ole dick."

She starts rocking slow, lifting herself up and dropping that ass back down. Each time she lands in my lap, I bite my lip to keep from moaning like a bitch. Then she picks up speed.

Clap. Clap. Clap. Clap.

The bottom of her cheeks smacks against my thighs. I grab one of her saggy tits and start sucking on it. She grabs the back of my head and explodes all over my dick.

"Oh my gawd… I'm cumming! I'm cummminng!"

Her walls clamp down around me. I grip her ass, peeling her cheeks apart while I work my hips.

Squelch. Squelch. Squelch.

Her snatch is disgustingly wet. My balls tighten as I feel a massive nut coming on. Sweat runs down my brow, but Sharday leans in and licks it off my forehead. My nut sack is drenched, her juices sliding down the crack of *my* ass.

"Fuck, I'm finna cum, I'm finna cum!" I growl, more of a warning than a proclamation.

Click… click.

The bolts on the front door unlatch. Keys jingle. *Tink's back.*

I'm too far gone to react or even care. "Fuck… fuck… fuck… here it cummmsss!"

Right before I shoot my load up in Sharday, my dick slips out, and warm nut splashes across her ass cheeks.

"Oh shit, my bad," Tink says as she walks in, catching the whole show. Just knowing she's watching makes my dick spit even more. Spurts decorate Sharday's golden globes.

Sharday eyes Tink, smiles, and slips me back inside her. I don't know if it's the coke or her pussy, but my shit stays bricked. Before I know it, she's cumming on me again. Somewhere in the background, I hear Tink's bedroom door open and close. *I hope she doesn't feel disrespected about us getting down in her living room.*

I make Sharday stand up, bend over the arm of the sofa, and slide back in. For the next hour, I fuck the dog shit out of her dopefiend ass. No cap, she's got some of the best pussy I've ever had. I didn't know what "multi-orgasmic" meant until Sharday came on my dick ten times in an hour.

After I nut for the third time, we finally take a break. That's when the guilt and shame kick in. *I just fucked a smoker… raw.* I pray she didn't give me anything, if she did, that's another body on the list.

Now, all I want is a shower. Only problem? I gotta go through Tink's room to get to the bathroom.

Sharday lays sprawled on the couch, exhausted, while I make my way to Tink's bedroom door. I expect it to be locked, but when I twist the knob, it creaks open.

"Tink?… Tink?"

I poke my head in, but she looks asleep, or maybe just laid up under the covers. I decide not to wake her.

I tiptoe past the bed, grab a fresh pair of boxers, a wife beater, a face towel, and a bath towel, then hop in the tub. When I finish and come back into the room, the bed's empty.

What the fuck?

I get dressed and head to the living room, Sharday's gone too.

Weird.

I drop onto the couch and notice a bag of dope on the coffee table. I stare at it for a few seconds before dumping the contents out. I make two fat lines and, even though I know I shouldn't, I snort them both.

The euphoria hits quick. Before I realize it, the sun's coming up, Tink's still gone… and so is the rest of the bag.

Claudia

I'm so excited, today's the first time I'll get to spend with Kay since picking him up from the County jail. He told me he relocated to the outskirts of the city but didn't want to say exactly where. Last night, I got a few texts from him, letting me know how bad he wanted to spend the day with me.

Luckily, Harrell's working a long shift. I called in sick as soon as I got up this morning. Lance already hinted that I'll have to "pay" for that when I see him Saturday. *I can only imagine what sadistic shit he has planned for me.*

The second Harrell walks out the door, I run upstairs to get ready. First stop, the spa. I need a complete, full-body wax. From our many talks while he was locked up, I know Kay doesn't like his woman hairy.

After the spa, I hit the bank. Even though he didn't ask, I want to take him shopping. My plan is to withdraw ten grand. Only problem? Harrell and I have a security feature on our joint accounts, neither of us can withdraw more than five without the other's written consent.

Since he works a lot, we set it up so he can give consent over the phone. Earlier this morning, I lied to my husband. I told him my grandparents back in Columbia had gotten into some financial trouble and needed the money. Naively, he didn't even ask what kind of trouble. His trust in me is overwhelming. Since I barely ever ask for money, he didn't hesitate to call the bank and give his consent.

Once I get back to the house, I get dressed and call Kay. As the phone dials, I check myself in the full-length mirror.

Black and silver Fendi tennis skirt with the matching top, four-inch Fendi heels, I know I'm looking scrumptious.

I top it off with light jewelry, a white diamond tennis bracelet, a white diamond ladies' Rolex, and a pair of diamond-studded earrings. I'm lookin' like the boss bitch I am. I want to make sure that on our first official date, Kay is proud to have me on his arm.

"Hello?"

My heart skips a beat when I hear his voice tickle my eardrum. "Hey, babe, what time you want me to come scoop you up?"

"Shit, really, you can come pull up right now if you want."

I glance at my watch, *3:37 p.m.* "Well, text me your location and I'll be on the way."

"Bet!"

We hang up. Seconds later, my phone chimes. I get the location and type it in, Google Maps says it's I-10 East, close to Baytown. I hop inside my Porsche truck and make my way over there. The whole drive, I'm thinking about how I can really show Kay what I truly desire from a man. I need him to conquer the darkest parts of me, to dominate and master me in every way possible. *That's* the only way I can be happy in a relationship.

After twenty minutes, I exit the freeway and make a left under I-10. When I pull up to his house, I'm impressed. Even though it isn't as big as Harrell's and mine, it's still impressive for a man who hasn't been out of prison ninety days yet.

I park and text him that I'm outside. Kay: *Cum inside.*

I step out and walk toward the front door. The neighborhood feels peaceful. I can't help but wonder, *What would it feel like to live out here?*

Before I can knock, the door swings open, and my panties instantly flood. Standing in the doorway is a living god. Black Gucci denim shorts with a green-and-white Gucci belt, sagging just enough to show the red-and-green Gucci band on his boxers. On his feet, mid-top white-and-black Gucci sneakers with green G's peppered all over them.

But that's not what gets me. He has the nerve to be shirtless, tattoos covering his torso, muscles bulging, looking like a thugged-out action figure. *This man is too goddamn fine.*

"Come in, I'm almost ready," he says, stepping aside. I walk past him, making sure to put an extra twist in my hips.

"You want something to drink?"

"It depends. Do *you* want me to have something to drink?"

Kay shrugs. "Shit, you're the one driving."

I don't answer. I want him to *tell* me to have a drink. He doesn't. Instead, he heads upstairs to finish getting dressed. I take the time to check his place out.

Understandably, it's bare. The furniture is nice but scarce. *He definitely needs a woman's touch.*

Moments later, he appears. "Ready?"

"Whenever you are," I reply, and we both head outside.

I instinctively walk to the passenger side. He looks at me inquisitively but doesn't say anything. As soon as we get inside, I hand him the keys along with the bank envelope I pulled from my purse.

Kay looks confused. "What's this?"

"A welcome-home present. I thought you might want to buy a few things, but it's yours to do with however you see fit," I assure him.

He smiles. "Damn, Claw, you sure know how to make a nigga feel good."

"As long as you allow me to, I'll always do what I must to please you."

He doesn't reply. Instead, he cranks the engine, and we take off. We end up at the Galleria, but instead of spending the money on himself, Kay picks out a few pieces of lingerie he wants to see me in.

As we're leaving the mall, we pass a group of men waiting on valet and overhear them talking about an upscale lounge called Riley's.

"What you think, you wanna hit it?" Kay asks.

"Whatever you choose, Daddy, I will follow."

Kay eyes me suspiciously, no doubt wondering why every time he asks for my opinion, my answer's always along those same lines.

"Okay, well type it in your phone and see where it's located."

Turns out, the lounge is right outside of Houston. Jersey Village to be exact. We arrive around *5:30* in the evening and are surprised to see the parking lot packed.

We walk in and the atmosphere instantly has us feeling some type of way.

"What you wanna dri—" Kay stops mid-sentence. Instead of asking, he brings me back what *he* wants me to have. *Now he's getting it.*

After the second drink, I'm feeling frisky. I notice the same small group of men from the mall standing on the side of the bar.

"Daddy, do you want to dance?"

"Naw, I'm good. But if you want to, go ahead."

"Do you want me to?" I challenge.

Kay stares me dead in my eyes. I see his sparkle with understanding. *He finally gets it.*

He grabs me by the chin, lifts my head up, and says, "I want you to go out there, find you a nigga, then bounce that fat ass on him."

I tremble with excitement. My panties are sticking to my sex lips.

I turn around and survey the dance floor, looking, searching, until my eyes land on the same group from the mall. I walk up to the tall, dark one. Six-foot-two, dark skin, taper fade. I grab his hand and lead him into a corner.

"Damn, momma, I see you 'bout bidness."

You don't know the half of it.

I shove him against the wall and back that ass up until I feel his print poking at me. With my eyes locked on Kay, I twerk, roll, and work that ass in dude's lap.

I feel his hands creep up under my skirt. I *should* say something, but I'm too worked up to give a fuck. His grip tightens on my thighs. His dick's hard, nestled between my ass cheeks.

"Damn, baby, you got a nigga going crazy back here," he huffs.

His right-hand inches closer to my panty-clad coochie. I moan as I grind even harder on his dick.

Finally, he slips my panties to the side and, with one long finger, starts diddling my clit. Instantly, I buckle. By the look on Kay's face, he knows something has changed, though he doesn't know to what degree. As far as he knows, I could be getting fucked right here on the dance floor.

Still, he sits back and watches the show. I work my hips while dude works my clit. Kay licks his lips, seeing the ecstasy on my face, and I explode all over dude's fingers.

I reach back, squeeze my dance partner's thighs, and squeeze my nut out. *Whhooo ssshhhit!* That was an intense nut, especially with no penetration.

Dude removes his hand, licks his fingers clean, and leans in to whisper in my ear, "Damn, momma, what I gotta do to get the full course?"

I don't respond. Instead, I pull my panties back in place, smooth out my skirt, and head back to Kay. After seeing me in action, he's got a better understanding of what I need and desire.

As I approach, he holds my drink out. I take it and down the rest in one gulp. My coochie's on fire. I want so bad to pull his dick out and give him head in front of the whole club, but I wouldn't dare move unless he told me to.

I stand there, waiting for his next instructions, but he hesitates. I can almost see his mind working. *He doesn't know how far to go, or what my limits are.*

Soon, he'll realize I have none.

Suddenly, he gets an idea. "Claw, you see that nigga over there? The one in the black dress shirt?"

I let my eyes travel down his line of sight. "Yes, Daddy, I see him."

"I want you to take him in a corner, jack his dick, but don't let him cum until I give you the signal."

"And what's the signal, Daddy?"

"When I rub my face, that's the signal."

My whole body's tingling, knowing Kay and I are finally on the same page. He has me ready to explode. I do as he commands.

Dude in the dress shirt is on the verge of popping his load for twenty minutes straight. Every time he's about to get relief, I squeeze the head and let him deflate. It gets to the point where he's screaming *torture*.

Finally, Kay gives me the signal. When dude finally does cum, his load shoots two feet in the air. He almost collapses. As he tries to thank me and exchange info, I walk off, heading straight back to my *Master*.

The rest of the night's pretty much the same. Once Kay sees it's getting close to that time, he decides we should head home. He's horny as hell and makes me suck his dick the whole ride back. I swallow his load twice before we pull into his driveway.

"I don't want you brushing your teeth until you kiss your husband tonight," he commands.

Of course, I agree.

I head home, finally feeling content for once. I have a man in my life who gives me exactly what I need. The only drawback is, I'm married to his brother.

I make it home, shower, making sure not to brush my teeth. I *could* have and just told Kay I didn't, but that wouldn't make me a true submissive. I want complete and utter dominance.

I whip up a quick meal, and by the time Harrell arrives, dinner's ready. I plant a nice, wet kiss on him as he walks through the door, giving him plenty of tongue. I notice him flinch. *I wonder if he'll say something.*

Of course, he doesn't. We eat, I wait for him to shower, then I take my sexual frustrations out on him. The whole time, I'm picturing his brother, already counting down until the next time we get together.

Chapter 8

Andrea

"Hello?"

"Hey girl, what you got going?"

"Nothing much, why? Wassup?"

"You got plans tonight?"

"Uh, not really."

"Well, me and my girl Mary are heading out. I'm trying to see if maybe you wanna ride." I can almost hear the smile on her face.

"Hell yeah. Where we going? What's the dress code?"

"Where else, Club Heat. And it's grown and sexy."

I know Alison's been dying to go out with me. Last time she did, we were with her sister Danielle and couldn't really cut up like we wanted. Now that she's fully grown, I'm about to show her how to *really* get active.

"Bet. What time?"

I check my Apple Watch. "We gone ride out about ten-thirty." Then a thought hits me. "Where you at?"

She stumbles over her words, then gets quiet. "Hello? Alison, you still there?"

"Yeah, I'm still—"

"So, where we need to come scoop you from?"

"Uhh... give me like five minutes. Let me holla at my homegirl real quick. I wanna make sure it's cool to give you, her address."

"Huh? Okay, well let me know something ASAP." *Yeah... she's definitely hiding something,* I tell myself. My mind goes back to the day I saw her carrying car keys with the shark emblem on the keychain. *Imma find out who you're fucking, lil' girl, and it better not be my baby daddy.*

Five minutes later, Alison calls me back. "Hello?"

"Hey, I talked to my girl and I'll just catch an Uber to where y'all at."

"An Uber? Why would you do that when we can just scoop you up on the way to the club?"

She doesn't have a logical answer.

"A'ight, if that's what you wanna do." I give her my address and tell her she needs to be here by nine-thirty so we can head out by ten.

We hang up and I get ready for a lemon bath. Afterwards, I douche, wax, and shave my legs. Once my makeup's flawless, I slip into my red Hermes mid-thigh dress AD bought me for our last anniversary. The top half is tight, but the bottom's loose, my ass too fat, the dress keeps climbing. I have to constantly keep pulling it down.

My phone vibrates. It's Alison, texting me to let me know she's on the way. I'm already trying to figure out how to siphon the truth out her ass. I know she's sitting on a big, fat, juicy secret, and I won't be able to sleep until I find out exactly what it is.

She pulls up around *9:15*, rocking a short-ass cream Bugatchi dress and four-inch Bottega heels. I know the lil' bitch ain't got no money, so whatever dick she's keeping wet must've bought it for her.

"Heyy, girl," she sings, as we hug.

I playfully tap her on the ass. "Girl, your ass getting too thick. Somebody must be dropping that dick off in your young ass," I tease.

She blushes, moving her bangs to the side. That's when I get a good look at her Bulgari wristwatch. *Oh, this bitch wanna flex!*

"Now, you know my boyfriend went back to school a while back. I haven't had sex since then," she claims. I can tell she's lying through her teeth, but I let it slide.

"Well, he must've been putting in work while he was here, 'cause it shows."

I can tell she's eager to change the subject, so I let her.

"So, who's this Mary you was telling me about?" Alison kicks off her heels and pops a squat on my couch.

"She's my girl. We met at my new job. She's Hispanic, but got flavor like a sistah," I tell her.

"Oh, okay. Well, I know if she's kicking it with you, she's good people."

"Fa'sho. You want something to drink?" I ask, heading to the kitchen. I'm one of those types who likes to get a lil' buzzed *before* I get to the club.

"Sure. How 'bout some Remy?"

"One Remy, coming up."

After we both get a lil' drink in our system, we head out to pick up Mary from her brother's crib. I'd dropped her off earlier, apparently they had some important business to discuss.

As soon as we pull up and Mary comes out, I can tell something's wrong. She takes one look at Alison, and her energy shifts. It never occurred to me that Alison being in the front seat might cause a problem.

Low-key, Mary and I are seeing each other. We haven't made it official, but it's understood, she's mine and I'm hers. Originally, the plan was for her and I to scoop up Alison *together. Shit... I hope this doesn't ruin the night.*

Mary looks at me for a second, waiting to see if I'll make Alison switch seats. When I don't, she opens the rear passenger door and gets in, huffing.

"Hey, girl," I greet her, eyeing her through the rearview mirror. My eyes plead for her to *chill out*.

"Hey, y'all," she responds—her eyes telling me *you done fucked up.*

"Mary, this my homegirl Alison. Alison, this my *girl* Mary."

Mary smirks at my slick way of trying to claim her, while still keeping it a secret.

It's not that I'm ashamed. One thing about me—I don't give a fuck what somebody thinks about me or the choices I make. It's just… I've never been in a relationship with a woman before, and I don't know the rules of engagement. Plus, I'm not a hundred percent sure I'm ready to make that claim just yet.

Alison turns around in her seat. "Nice to meet you."

"Likewise."

They shake hands, and I turn on some Sexy Redd to get us amped.

By the time we hit the club, I'm on go. We park and don't even make it five yards before a group of niggas shoot their shot. They're cute, and I wouldn't mind linking up, but Mary's not having it. Alison follows our lead, and the guys are left standing there, staring at our asses as we head inside.

Heat is off the chain, as usual. Twice a month, they unofficially have a *gay night*. Tonight, it's eighty percent women, and they all look good enough to eat.

We decide to pitch in for a V.I.P. booth. It comes with a complimentary bottle of champagne. We also agree to invite five people each, and twenty minutes later, our section's packed. A few of our guests buy us a couple bottles of Rosé to show appreciation. When I tell you we're lit, that's an understatement. One dark-skinned woman has her thumb halfway up a light-skinned woman's asshole. Then, we spot another thick, brown-skinned woman laid back on the couch, legs spread, getting feasted on by a chubby stud with a taper fade.

Don't get it twisted, there's a few straight men in the place too. The ones smart enough to do the math. Eighty percent women means there's a greater chance of going home with somebody. Add in the fact every woman is either bi or lesbian, and the chances of a threesome shoot through the roof.

I pay close attention to Alison. She's sitting on the couch with a big-booty redbone giving her a sensual lap dance. At first, she's laughing and joking around. But soon, she starts to get into it, biting her bottom lip as ole girl rolls and grinds in her lap.

Alison's so into it; she hasn't noticed her dress has crept up her thigh. Her cream-colored panties have a dark wet spot right where the mouth of her pussy's covered.

Just watching the scene has my own juices flowing. Instinctively, I search for Mary. She's in the corner, staring me down. I can tell by her face she's itching to get in my drawers. I glance at my watch, *1:37 a.m.* The club's about to close. She catches my vibe and comes over.

"You ready?" I ask, already knowing her answer.

"Hell yeah."

"Damn," I say, gesturing toward Alison. "I don't know where she'll want me to drop her off. She rode an Uber to the crib. I'm lit as fuck and I ain't tryna do all that driving."

"Fuck it, bring her back to the crib," Mary suggests. "Take her home in the morning."

I look at Mary skeptically. "You sure?"

"Yeah. At first, I wasn't feeling her all in my seat, but lil' momma cool as hell. Plus, she's cute to boot. So..." She gives me this conspiratorial look.

I glance back at Alison. Ole girl's got her titties out while Alison's sucking one of her nipples. *That* settles it.

Just as I'm heading over to tell her it's time to go, we hear commotion at the front door. I turn and catch two studs barging through the crowd, looking for somebody. Both are dark-complected, rocking taper fades, jewelry glistening on their necks and wrists.

The shorter one taps the other on the shoulder, then points toward the V.I.P. section. I follow their line of sight and realize they're looking at Alison. Before I can put two and two together, they storm toward us. Without permission, they cross the rope and roll up on Alison. By the time I realize she's in serious danger, it's too late.

Smack!

The tall stud smacks fire from the big-booty redbone giving Alison the lap dance. Ole girl tumbles sideways and lands on her back, legs in the air. We get an unobstructed view of her crotch—panties pushed to the side, lips slick, hole slightly dilated. *Alison must've been playing in that bitch's pussy.*

"Bitch, you think this shit a game. I knew you wasn't at your momma's house!" the stud roars.

Alison, clearly confused, tries to get up, but the shorter stud pushes her back down.

"Hoe, where you think you going?" she snarls.

Before Alison can jump up and defend herself, Marisol swings something at the shorter stud's head. I hear a dull *thunk* as the heel of her stiletto connects with flesh and bone.

"Awwww, sssshit!" the stud cries, blood starting to ooze from her head.

Her friend turns on my girl, about to step in, until I run over and catch her with a right hook to the side of the head.

"Bitch!" I yell as I connect.

Next thing I know, Alison hops off the couch and the three of us go to work on the tall stud. All you see is fists and stilettos raining down.

It doesn't take long for security to haul us off. My dress is halfway ripped. My left tit is out. One of the bouncers has Mary hemmed up by the waist, her skirt flipped up, exposing her bald cunt. All three of us are going haywire, trying to get loose, but they're too big and too strong.

Once we've been successfully thrown out, the cool night air caresses our frames, and we calm down immensely.

"Damn, girl, you fucked that hoe up in the Fendi heels," Alison compliments Mary.

Mary's holding the same heels in her hand, shaking her head. "Yeah, but I think I fucked my babies up though," she replies.

"Let me see," I tell her. She hands over the shoe. The heel looks flawless, but there's blood on the velvet. "Yeah… it's gon' be hell tryna get the blood out."

We hop in my car, feeling jubilant. This time, Alison slides in the backseat. *I wonder if she peeped something at the club.*

"So, what's the move now?" she asks as I crank up the engine.

"Well, we plan on heading home and just kicking it for the rest of the night."

"Oh." Alison's disappointment is obvious. No doubt she assumed when I said *we*, I meant just Mary and me.

"You don't have to be back home anytime soon, do you?" Mary asks.

"Oh naw, I'm good," Alison answers quickly, relieved.

"Well, three of us are going back to my place. If that's cool with you," Mary tells her.

"Of course."

I turn out of Club Heat's parking lot. Now the night officially begins.

We pull up to Mary's crib around *2:20 a.m.* She stays in a set of apartments off the Beltway called Alta Crossing. They're fairly new, and a lot of people been rushing to move into them. Mary just got out of jail a few months back, and even though she's got a big family, she prefers to stay by herself.

"Y'all want something to drink?" she asks.

"Sure," Alison and I say in unison.

We each fix a glass of Crown Royal and chat for a minute before Mary excuses herself to shower.

"I have a guest bath you can use. Plus, some clothes you can sleep in," Mary tells Alison.

Alison takes her up on the offer. I know Mary wants me to hop in with her, but I wait until she's done, then I get myself together.

Once all three of us are clean, we pour up another drink and sit around the living room chatting in t-shirts and panties. It doesn't take long for the liquor to kick in.

Mary's the first to make a move. She stands, walks over to me, drops to her knees, and takes my left foot in her tiny hand.

"I know your feet hurt, babe."

This is the first time either of us has used a term of endearment in front of Alison. Mary starts rubbing my feet the way I like, and soon I'm leaning back, letting her work.

After my feet are thoroughly massaged, her hands travel north until they reach my damp panties. Still staring into my eyes, Mary slides them down. I lift my ass off the couch so she can take them completely off. Once I'm bare-assed, she pushes my thighs back and further apart. My coochie pops out, opening up for her.

Mary snakes the tip of her tongue between my folds until she lands on my button.

"Fuuucck… ssshhhit!" I hiss as she suckles my clit. I grab the side of her head with my right hand, and with my left, I pull out my right tit and tweak my nipple.

My eyes flash to Alison. She's on the adjacent couch, staring intensely as Mary devours me. I bite my lip and, with my eyes, invite her to join. She doesn't move, but she doesn't look away.

"Oh shit, baby… you 'bout to make me cum. Fuck… I'm finna cuummm!"

I cry out as Mary sucks, slurps, and salivates all over my pussy. I jerk, then flood her mouth with cum. She moans into my coochie, drinking her fill, then stands.

I sit up and start pulling her panties down, inhaling her wet, needy scent. Once they're off, I lay on the floor and let her sit on my face.

Her pussy always tastes fresh and sweet to me. Her juices drip and cascade down my chin as I try to catch every drop. Attempts to look back, but I'm preventing her by holding her head in place. I know once she sees that monster, she'll be scared straight.

"Ssshh… don't worry 'bout it. Just keep eating this pussy," I coach her.

Alison squeezes her eyes shut as Mary starts sawing in and out, back and forth, back and forth. Once Mary finds her rhythm, Alison begins to shiver with pleasure. Mouth full of pussy, cunt full of rubber cock, Alison has her first mind-blowing orgasm of the night.

By now, Mary's hitting her with deep, powerful strokes. I hear Alison's pussy talking back. *Squelch, squelch, squelch. Wet noodle siracha.* She can barely keep her mouth glued to me, grunting and groaning as Mary works to turn her young ass out.

Suddenly, Alison lifts her head.

"Oh my gawd, oh my gawd… I'm finna cum again. Ssshit… fuuccckk… I'm cummmminnn!"

Mary holds onto Alison's hips and rides her down into the carpet. I slide back and let my girl put that work in. Sitting on the couch, I play in my pussy while Mary makes the young bitch tap out.

The rest of the night, Mary and I take turns flipping young Alison. By the time we all lay down, I'm sure she'll be fiending for a steady diet of pussy from now on. And trust, I'll be there to feed her when she hungers.

The next day, I wake up to find Alison gone, with a text on my phone:

Alison: *Caught an Uber. Had fun. Must do again.*

I text back: *Glad you had fun. Whenever you're ready.*

I put the phone down, turn over, and see Mary asleep, naked. I decide to wake her up with some good morning head.

Yeah... today will be a good day.

Rashard

"Hey babe, will you be home early tonight?"

"To be honest, I don't know. It all depends on what I come across at Bottoms Up," I tell Alison as I turn into the infamous strip club parking lot.

"Okay. Well, if I'm sleep, wake me up."

I know that trick. She wants me to wake her up so she can clock what time I come home—and see what state I'm in.

"I got you," I lie. Only way I'm waking her up is if I can't slide up in nothing wet tonight and need to get my rocks off.

We disconnect. I park, hop out my whip, and double-check myself in the reflection of my tint.

After the lick on Lil Mexico, I spent some bread upgrading my jewels. My yellow gold Patek Philippe, with canary diamonds flooding the bezel, is bussin'. My yellow gold Cuban with crushed diamonds has my neck shimmering. Add that to the fact I'm Louis Vuitton down to the ground, every bitch in the club will think I'm a D-Boy. But so will the niggas.

And that's exactly what I'm counting on. I pay the bouncer, Big Russ, and make my way inside. The scent of money and pussy invades my nostrils the second I step through the threshold. Bad bitches everywhere. To be real, I've never seen a busted-up chick at Bottoms Up. That's why every so-called made nigga or boss in the city comes here to get loose.

I head straight to the bar. The bartender's a big-booty yellow-bone named Deangela. I make sure I tip her good every time I come through. You know a nigga tryna slide up in her guts, but she keeps acting siddity.

She sees me and smiles. "Wassup, Rah, the usual?"

"Uh, not tonight. I'm trying something new."

"Okay. What'll it be then?"

I think for a second. "How 'bout a mixed drink? What you recommend?"

"Well, I like the White Russian."

"Make that two of them then."

After making my drinks, I give her a hundred-dollar bill. "Keep the change." The two drinks only total forty dollars.

I scan the club from behind the tints of my LV shades. As a jackboy, you gotta master the art of looking without looking, appear oblivious, but at the same time, obvious.

As I'm scoping the scene, a few strippers pull up, trying to see if they can squeeze a couple coins outta me. I turn the first few down, something any self-respecting D-Boy would do.

But when a thick redbone stripper named Strawberry pulls up, I let her take me to the private dance area. I use her as cover while I nonchalantly collect intel from other niggas in the vicinity.

Suddenly, a trio of niggas walk in, shining like the Michael Jackson glove. The atmosphere shifts, quiet buzz running through the strippers. *These niggas must be important.*

They get ushered straight into V.I.P. before they even sit down, two buckets of champagne waiting on them.

"Who's them niggas?" I ask Strawberry.

She turns around. "Oh, they some D-Boys from outta state. The one with the black and gold Versace shirt? That's Benny. He's the one with the money. The other two are more like his bodyguards," she says, with disdain.

The way she says it, either they curved her or tossed her around like a softball and left her outside in the grass.

Jackpot. I've found my next lick, I just need to figure out how to get close enough.

I give Strawberry another forty for two more lap dances while I plan my next move. I watch. I wait. Then it comes—one of the *bodyguards* is sweet on Deangela. Keeps coming in and out of V.I.P., stalking her at the bar.

Once the song ends, I push Strawberry off me and make my way over.

"What's good, Rah? You want another White Russian?"

"Not right now, but I got a proposition for you."

She gives me a look. "Uhh… what you talking 'bout, Rah?"

"Not that type of proposition, Angie. I got five hundred dollars for you if you put me in the door with them cats in V.I.P."

Her eyebrows shoot up, then she squints. "Rah, what the hell you got going on?"

"Ain't nothing like that, Angie. I need a new connect. I'm hearing dude's heavy and might be the one to talk to."

Good thing I don't let everyone know my true self. If Deangela knew who I *really* was, she'd never connect me. Lucky for me, she doesn't, so she does.

"All I gotta do is introduce y'all and I get five hundred dollars?" she asks, still skeptical.

I nod. "That's it. Just introduce me. Think you can get me to Benny?"

"Well, I don't know 'bout Benny. Him and I barely talk. His homeboy Cinco's the one who's always pulling up on me."

"Okay, well just do what you can, and I got you."

She agrees. I post up on the stool at the end of the bar, playing on the machine. Doesn't take long for Cinco to come up, this time for five thousand ones. After Angie gets the manager to *change him out*, I peep them through my peripheral, talking in the corner. She nods subtly in my direction. Dude stares at me for a couple seconds before turning back toward her and saying a few words. Angie grabs his hand seductively before he walks back toward V.I.P.

After he's gone, she approaches.

"So, what's the verdict?" I inquire.

"I told him you were like family and needed a genuine plug. Crazy thing is, he said Benny's looking for somebody stomp-down he can work with."

"So now what?"

"He said he's gonna holla at him and let him know," she says.

I was hoping for an introduction right then and there, but I'll have to be patient. I go back to playing on the machine for the rest of the night. Nothing transpires.

Fifteen minutes before the club closes, Benny and his boys start making their way out. I'm thinking they passed on the opportunity, until I see Cinco approach Angie and exchange words. After a few seconds, she calls me over.

"Hey Rah, this my friend Cinco. Cinco, this my people Rah."

Cinco extends his hand. "Wassup, homie."

I shake his hand.

"Angie tells me you're looking for a solid plug."

"Hell yeah. My last plug got killed, and I've been scraping by ever since."

"What you be fucking with?"

"Really, ain't shit I can't move, but I fucks with the snow," I tell him.

"Well, what about Tar?"

"I've dibbled and dabbled, but I ain't never had a steady flow."

Cinco nods in understanding. "Well, my nigga Benny wants to meet you real quick."

I can't hide the smile. "Right now?"

"Yeah. We 'bout to make a move, and he wants to rap with you before we bounce." Cinco turns to Angie. "A'ight, baby girl, I'll catch up with you tomorrow."

"You do that," she purrs.

After he leaves, I look at her suspiciously.

"What? That's how I made it happen for you. That nigga been hounding me for my number the last couple weeks. I figured, for five hundred dollars, he can have it."

She extends her hand, palm up. I hand her five crisp hundred-dollar bills.

"You better hurry up before them niggas burn off."

I rush outside and spot Cinco next to a cocaine-white Cadillac Escalade on 28“ white Forgis. He sees me, calls me over, and opens the back door for me to get in.

Sitting there, playing on his phone, is Benny. He doesn't even look my way as I slide in next to him.

"My people tell me you're looking for a plug."

"Yeah, I am."

"What's your usual quota?"

Now, I'm not a hustler, so I've never handled big weight, unless I peeled a nigga for his shit. But I know if I want him to take me seriously, I gotta make myself worth the investment.

"I'm used to running through five bricks every two weeks, but that's 'cause I buss it down. If I had a steady supplier, I could expand, probably flush fifty bricks a month."

Benny finally looks my way. "What about Tar?"

"Like I told Cinco, I never got in deep with that, but we can start off light. Once I build the clientele, we can go heavy. Look, I'm in this for the long haul. If you can guarantee me a steady flow, I can guarantee it'll get gone."

Benny studies me for what feels like forever, like he's wrestling with a decision.

"You got an ID?" he finally asks.

"Huh?"

"ID. Driver's license?"

"Yeah… why, wassup?"

"Let me see it."

I look at him confused, but he's still staring at me expectantly. I pull my license out and hand it to him. He snaps a picture of it with his phone.

"Man, what the fuck? What type of shit you on?" I wasn't expecting that.

"Insurance purposes. I'll do a background check. Long as you come back clean, I'll be in touch."

He hands me back my ID. Cinco opens the door for me to get out.

As they pull out the parking lot, I stand there confused, unsure what to do next. What I do know, when it's time to move on dude, Imma have to be extra cautious. I see now, this nigga plays for keeps. I debate on going back home, but I spot Strawberry coming out with her bags. Baby girl thick as fuck. I got a couple hundred to blow, courtesy of Lil Mexico, so I pull up on her with a proposition. After some tough negotiating, she agrees to let me jump up and down in her pussy for three hundred and fifty dollars. *Damn, that's less than I paid Alison for the meet and greet.*

By the time we make it to the room, I forget all about Benny and spend the rest of the night making Strawberry shake.

Chapter 9

Kelsey

Tap, tap, tap.

I'm parked in these run-down apartments called Maxey Village. Soon as I pull in and park, this dark-skinned dude dressed in all red walks up and taps on my window. *Tap, tap, tap.* From the bulge under their shirts, I can tell him, and his homie are strapped.

I cautiously roll my window down. He leans in.

"Who you over here for?" the taller of the two asks.

The other one's busy looking all inside my car, like he's checking for somebody hiding on the floorboard.

"Uhh, I'm here for Brazy Nut," I say in my most suburban, white-girl voice. I've learned when dealing with hood niggas, it's best to seem white and naïve as possible. For some reason, when I do that, their defenses and aggression taper down.

"Oh, okay."

He steps away from the car and pulls out his phone, calling Brazy to verify. Meanwhile, his friend uses the chance to get a better look at me. With these daisy-duke coochie cutters on, all he sees is legs and thighs. His eyes land on my camel toe, the hungry look in them gives me chills.

"Where you from? I ain't never seen you around here. You got some homegirls?"

Before I can answer, the taller one comes back and tells me I'm good to go. I can't wait to get out this car and away from these two. Don't get me wrong, I love mine rough and rugged, but something about these two gives me the creeps. Especially the shorter one.

As I hop out, my shorts ride up the crack of my ass. Even though I don't want to do it in front of them, I reach back and pull them out. *Damn, that white bitch fine,* I hear one of them say as I bend the corner.

I find Brazy's apartment and knock on the door. *Knock, knock, knock.*

Brazy opens up, and a cloud of smoke escapes from the small apartment. The weed aroma is strong as hell. He's standing there in Givenchy shorts, no shirt, torso covered in ink, rocking two gold chains and a gold-and-diamond-studded watch.

"I see you didn't get lost," he jokes, stepping aside.

I walk in and notice two other dudes in the living room. I turn toward Brazy.

"Damn, I ain't know you had company."

"When you called, I didn't. These two just pulled up,"he claims.

Something tells me he's lying through his teeth. I've been fucking with hood niggas long enough to know when I'm being set up for a possible train situation.

I don't call him out. Instead, I head over to the open spot on the couch.

"You smoke?" Brazy asks.

"Sometimes."

He grabs a blunt wrap off the coffee table and starts twisting one up. I take a moment to check out the other two guests. One's tall, with copper-red skin. His eyes are light brown, and his lips look succulent and juicy. The other's short and stocky, milk-chocolate complexion, with a set of spinning waves. Each of 'em tatted up like Brazy.

All three of them can get it, on the cool, I muse to myself, watching them battle on *2K*.

"Here."

Brazy hands me the blunt to spark. Honestly, I'm not a big smoker. I prefer liquor to weed, but right now I'll do anything to accomplish my mission. I light the blunt, pull, and damn near bust a lung.

Awka, awka, awka.

I cough up a storm. Brazy and his boys can't stop laughing.

"Damn, lil' momma, you gotta be careful with that. That's rapper weed."

As soon as he says it, my whole body starts tingling. I feel warm and fuzzy all over. My kitty starts to moisten. I try to pass it, but Brazy insists I take another hit. *Slick ass.*

This time, I don't pull as hard, but I hold it in longer. I still cough, but not as violently. By the time it makes it back to me, I'm stoned out my motherfucking mind. I can barely keep my eyelids open.

I feel Brazy sit down next to me. Then, his lips are on my neck, kissing and sucking.

"Oooh, ssshhhit," I hear myself moan.

His hand slides straight to my cunt, rubbing on it through my denim.

"Game, nigga! I told you; you can't fuck with me, especially when I got them Nuggets," one of his homeboys blurts out.

I force my eyes open. Apparently, the bright one won the game, and now he's demanding payment. The darker one reaches in his pocket and hands him a bill.

Red looks at it, face twisting. "Nigga, what's this?"

"What you mean, what's this?" the darker one replies.

"Tron, we bet a hundred. This a twenty. Where the rest of my bread at?"

"Nigga, we ain't bet no hundred. I asked if you wanna bet a dollar, you ain't say shit. So, we bet what we been betting, twenty!"

Even as high and horny as I am, I know shit's about to get ugly, quick.

Red stares Tron down for a second, then in one fluid motion, pulls his strap.

"Whoa, whoa, whoa." Brazy finally tears himself away from feeling me up. "Both of you niggas tripping. Drako, put the gun down, homie, before you do something you'll regret."

"Maaan, fuck all that, Blood. Ain't no hoe in me. That nigga bet a hundred. He lost, so he needs to pay up," Drako spits with venom.

"Okay, I agree. But you know once them *thangs* come out, ain't no good can come from it. Just put the gun down, so we can come to a solid conclusion," Brazy says, trying to calm him.

"Dawg, it's only one conclusion, he gon' pay me the rest of my money."

"How much he owes you, Blood?"

"Eighty dollars."

"Okay… how 'bout I pay the eighty and get bro to shoot *me* the bread back."

A way out. I see the relief in Drako's face as his anger starts to seep away.

He turns toward Brazy. "Damn, bro, a nigga ain't—""

Thwack!

Tron cracks him across the jaw with a solid right hook. The pistol flies from Drako's hand as he crashes through the sheetrock, leaving a colossal hole in the wall. Amazingly, he's not knocked out. He sees Tron scrambling for the pistol. Instead of trying to beat him to it, Drako jumps up and makes a dash for the door.

Seconds later, Tron chases after him, pistol at his side.

My high is completely blown.

"What the fuck?" I look at Brazy, confused.

As soon as he starts to answer, we hear the dreadful sound of gunshots.

Bocka! Bocka! Bocka!

We lock eyes.

I grab my phone and run for the door, Brazy right on my heels. Around the breezeway, into the parking lot, I nearly trip over Drako's body.

He's laid out, upper body wedged between two cars, lower half sprawled on the sidewalk. One of the cars has blood and brain matter dripping off the front wheel well. Brazy tries to pick him up, but we see half the back of his head is gone.

Damn!

I quickly hop in my whip. Brazy jumps in the passenger seat. I want to tell him, *Where the fuck you think you going?* Instead, I crank the engine, throw it in reverse, and get the hell off the scene.

As soon as we're a block away, I turn to him. "Where you want me to drop you off at?"

He looks at me, confused. "Drop me off? I thought we was gonna finish what we started."

I stare at him like he just fell off the turnip truck. "Finish what we started? I just seen a dude with his brains all over the parking lot, and you think I'm still in the mood?"

Brazy looks at me like seeing a dead body is just another re-run of *Law & Order*. He's about to say something when his phone rings.

"Hello? Naw, don't swang through, I'm in traffic right now. Yeah, something popped off at the spot. I'll tell you 'bout it face-to-face. Uhh, hold up."

Brazy puts the phone down and looks at me. "You feel like taking me to meet up with my nigga Tori B, real quick?"

Tori B? Ain't he the one that's cool with Andrea's baby daddy?

"Sure. Where's he at?"

Brazy hops back on the phone. "Yeah, I can meet you… uhh, okay. Give us like seven minutes. Bet!"

Once he hangs up, he tells me to take him to Carl's B.B.Q. Even though it's closed, it's a safe place to park and talk.

When we pull up, I spot a canary-yellow Benz 550. I park next to it. Brazy looks like he's about to hop out and jump in Tori's whip, but instead, Tori gets out to greet him. I'm glad he does. Where Brazy is wild and irrational, Tori is calm and cunning.

Five-foot-ten, one-eighty, spinning waves and a dazzling smile. He's draped in jewels and definitely has the aura of a boss. As he walks up to the passenger side, our eyes lock.

"How you doing, Ms. Lady? I apologize if I ruined y'all's evening."

"Oh, trust me, this evening was already over with. But thank you anyway,"I assure him.

"You mind if I get in?"

"Sure."

I unlock the door, and he hops in my backseat. As him and Brazy go over the events of the night, I keep catching him glancing at me in the rearview. *Yes, I will be getting at him.* I just don't know how, until the opportunity presents itself.

I yawn.

Tori, being the perceptive man he is, asks, "We're not having you out too late, are we? I know you must be a working woman. I don't want you to be late to work and fuck up your bag."

"Oh naw, you good. I work at the department store on Wallisville and the Beltway. Don't have to be in until ten a.m." I give him a look as I finish my sentence. Tori nods in understanding. *Now, the ball's in his court.*

Once the two finish their business, Tori gets out, and I turn to Brazy. "Where you want me to drop you off at?"

He looks disappointed but finally says, "Drop me off at my baby momma crib."

If he thinks I'm about to be upset about that, he's mistaken.

"Where she stay?"

"Coolwood."

That means we gotta go back down Maxey to get to Federal Road, then turn down Fleming. I'm not exactly excited about it, but I'm eager to get him out of my car.

As we head down Maxey, I can see from a hundred yards away, police have the whole Maxey Village blocked off as a crime scene. Passing by, I spot yellow tape and a forensic team moving around. Flashbacks of Drako's head blown open hit me.

It's crazy how they could've both been balls-deep in some pussy, but instead, over eighty dollars, one's dead, and the other's scared.

I drop Brazy off, despite his insistence that we get a room "real quick."

"Naw, baby boy, I gotta work tomorrow," I tell him.

"But you just said you wasn't tripping, and that you don't have to be to work until ten a.m.,"he points out.

"Yeah, but I gotta take care of something before I head in. Don't worry, we'll link up soon."

"When?" He almost sounds sad.

"I'll let you know,"I say as I peel off, leaving Brazy standing outside his baby momma's apartment.

As soon as I get home, I shower and get ready for bed. *Ain't no way I'm missing work tomorrow.*

Danielle

"Danielle, was it the woman in the green car that needed the potato salad?" my coworker Patrice asks as we get ready to carry out our orders.

Patrice started three weeks ago. So far, she seems cool. Cuban and Black, with good hair, banana-red complexion, curves for days, and a slight Spanish accent. *A bitch would have to watch her man around Patrice.*

"Yeah, girl, she wanted two orders of potato salad and one order of mac and cheese," I tell her.

"Okay, I thought so. I just wanted to be sure. Appreciate it."

"No problem, girl. I, oh shit!" I set the tray down on a nearby table. My lil' boy just mule-kicked my ass.

"Danielle, you good? You want me to fill your orders for you?" Patrice offers.

As tempting as it sounds, I decline. "Naw, girl, I got it. I just need a minute."

I'm six and a half months along and just found out I'm having a bad-ass lil' boy. Haven't decided on a name yet, but every day that passes, I fall more and more in love with him.

At first, I wanted Rah to be in his life. But now? I'm like *fuck him*. I'll hold my son down, one deep if I have to.

Once my lil' man stops with the soccer practice, I head outside to take my customers their order. They tip me a twenty. *Probably 'cause I'm pregnant.*

I'm on my way back inside when another car pulls up, a brand new, metallic-blue Range Rover. I walk up to the driver's side and damn near lose my breath. Sitting there is the most gorgeous man I've ever seen. I can't see his eyes behind his Fendi shades, but his jewelry can't be denied—neck, wrist, and fingers all sparkling in the sunlight.

"Welcome to Carl's. You already know what you want, or you need a menu?"

He studies me from behind those tinted lenses. "How 'bout a baked potato, with a side of blackberry cobbler."

"Good choice," I tell him as I head back inside to place the order.

The whole walk, I'm fighting the urge to look back. Naturally, pregnancy made me gain some weight. My belly's bigger, but so is my ass and thighs—bussing out the seams of my jeans. And my boobs? Twice their normal size.

I give the cashier *Mr. Range Rover's* order.

"Damn, girl, who's that in the Range? I can see his ice sparkle from all the way over here," Patrice says while filling an order for her customer.

"I don't know, but I plan to find out," I answer with fake confidence.

"Well, if you can snatch his ass up, see if he's got a friend."

"You know I got you."

They bring out our orders and I head back outside, nervous as hell.

Bitch, he's not gonna wanna talk to you. You big as a house. I scold myself.

I walk up to his window. "Here you go, sir. That'll be ten dollars and forty-six cents."

He hands me a fifty. "Keep the change, and it's Sosa Bay, not *sir*."

I smile. "Okay, Sosa Bay. Thank you for the tip."

"No problem. But I gotta be completely honest with you—I was hoping to grab your number for that generous tip."

I play mock offended. "What type of woman you take me for? Just gon' trick out my number like that?"

"Well, I apologize. I'm just a man who believes, if I see something I really want, I gotta be willing to pay for it, whatever the payment is."

"Sooo, what are you tryna say? You *really want* my number?"

He bites his bottom lip. "To be honest, I want more than that. But for now, the number will do."

His confidence and audacity got me soaking wet. That's why I love boss niggas; they don't mince their words.

"Well, I guess I can give you, my number. But don't have me waiting for your call and you don't use it."

I regret saying it as soon as it leaves my lips, the last thing I want is to look like some thot-ass bopper.

"Naw, baby girl, Imma hit you up. Matter fact, what you got planned tonight?"

"Nothing much. Just kicking it at the crib."

"Well, if you want, I can come kick it with you."

Damn, this nigga isn't playing. He called my bluff. If I turn him down now, I'll look like I'm all talk.

"Sure, we can do that. But you don't even know my name."

"Yes, I do."

I freeze, scanning his face for recognition. He sees my apprehension, smiles, and says, "It's on your name tag."

I look down and laugh. "Oh yeah, duh!"

"Yeah… we gon' definitely have to relieve your stress tonight," he coos. I swallow the lump in my throat. *Damn, this nigga got me creaming just off his approach. I haven't had a man aggressively pursue me like this in a long time.*

As he pulls out of the parking lot, I damn near want to pump my fist in the air. You know you're a bad bitch when you're out of shape, baby in the bun, and can still pull you a boss nigga.

5:30 comes quick. I clock out and practically run out of Carl's.

I stop by the grocery store and grab a few things to cook. I don't know what he likes, so I keep it simple, fried chicken, mac and cheese, and a quick 7Up cake. After I shower and hit myself with some smell good, I get a text from him. I send back my address, and he's on the way.

A bitch wants to jump sexy, but being pregnant, there's not much I can do fashion-wise. I settle on a pair of sweats and a sports bra. He knows I'm pregnant, so I see no point in trying to hide my bump. I hate wearing panties, but since I got pregnant my coochie stays wet. If I don't wear something to catch my juices, they'd be running down my leg all day.

I check my watch, *10:42*. I almost grab my phone to see where he's at. *I hope he ain't catch cold feet on a bitch.* Just as I'm about to call, it rings.

"Hello?"

"I'm outside."

"I'm in apartment 137. First one to the right when you come down the walkway."

"Bet." I hear his car door open through the phone. *"I'll see you in a sec."*

"Okay."

My nerves start to crackle. I don't understand why I'm acting like this. He's not the first man of his caliber I've messed with. Maybe it's because I'm so far along in my pregnancy. The fact that he still wants to fuck with me has me wanting to lock him down. And him being breaded up doesn't hurt. You never know, if I can lock him in, he might be willing to help me raise my son.

Knock, knock, knock.

I take a deep breath and open the door. Now that he's *standing* in front of me, I get the full dose. Five-foot-eleven, a hundred and ninety-something pounds, decked out in Givenchy from head to toe, rocking a gold bust-down Rolex as his only jewelry.

"Come in, come in. Welcome to mi casa," I tell him before he wraps me in a hug. I catch a whiff of his cologne and almost moan in his ear. *Damn, this man got me going.*

I glance at his face, once again, he's rocking shades. This time, Versace. I want to tell him to take them off so I can see his eyes. *Maybe later.*

"Damn, girl, something smells good."

"Yeah, I went ahead and whipped up a lil' something. I hope you eat fried chicken."

"What? Girl, don't you see the color of my skin? Of course I eat fried chicken. You got some hot sauce?"

"Boy, don't you see the color of *my* skin? Of course I got hot sauce. Matter fact, what kind you like?"

After grabbing him a bottle of Louisiana Hot Sauce, we sit down and get our grub on.

I learn he's from Missouri and has been in Texas less than a year. Claims he has no girls and no kids, but that remains to be seen.

When we're done, I clear the table and put on a movie. I'm an action junkie, so we settle on *John Wick 4.*

Halfway through, Sosa Bay makes his move. His hand slides into my sweats, finding my cotton panties drenched.

Laying back against his chest, I feel his dick rise, poking my lower back. From the feel of it, he's definitely packing heavy hardware. His fingers slip inside my panties, playing in my slushy.

"Hmmm," I moan as he dips two fingers in my cunt.

"Damn, girl, your shit super-soaker wet. You gon' let a nigga dig up in that, or what?"

"Uhh-huh," I moan, ready to get active.

"Stand up."

I get off the couch, standing in front of him, waiting on my next instruction. He pulls my sweats down. I step out of them. Next comes my soaked cotton panties.

"Man, your shit is out-of-control wet," he whispers to my coochie. I'm trembling with anticipation.

"Here, lay down for me."

He gets off the couch, and I stretch out in his spot. He places my left leg over the back of the couch and props my right over his shoulder. I look down at his head as it disappears beneath my belly, then I feel his tongue slither between my folds.

"Sssshit, baby… damn," I hiss as it flickers across my swollen nub.

Sosa smacks on my snatch, pulling at my meaty pussy lips.

"Mmmh… suck on that pussy, baby," I urge.

His lips wrap around my clit and pull, while his tongue swipes left to right, up and down, circling me over and over. Sweat forms on my brow. My nut starts to build. My toes curl and pop.

"Agghhh… ssshhit!" I grit my teeth as I cum all over his face.

"Whooo… shit… gawd damn!" I shiver while he slurps up my thick, creamy nut.

Suddenly, he stands and strips down to his socks. His dick's a good eight and a half inches, with a slight curve to the left. I make a move to sit up, but he stops me.

"Naw, baby… stay put. I want you to conserve your energy."

He kneels next to my head and presents his dick for me to feed on.

I gulp him down, pre-cum coating my taste buds. My left hand grabs his ass while my right keeps his dick steady.

Ghlup, ghlup, ghlup, ghlup.

Sosa fucks my throat with nice, steady strokes. It doesn't take long before his rod jerks in my mouth.

"Fuck, I'm finna cum, baby. You gon' swallow all this for me?"

Oh shit… I didn't plan to.

I've got a baby in my stomach, so I'm careful about what I take in. I don't answer, so Sosa basically gives me an ultimatum.

"I need you to eat that nut for me. I don't like for *my* bitch to spit out my seeds."

I close my eyes and nod *yes*.

Seconds later, he tilts his head back and growls, "Here it cums… here it cums… eat that nut, baby, eat all that shit. Aggghhh… fuuuuck!"

Instantly, my mouth fills with warm, gooey cock snot. I let it pool in my mouth, hesitant to swallow, until I open my eyes and see Sosa staring down at me expectantly. With one loud gulp, I swallow his entire load and pray my son will forgive me.

"That's a good girl… swallow every last drop."

I squeeze his dick, and the last remnant of cum squirts out his piss hole. I lick him clean, then suck him until he regains his hard form. Sosa pulls out of my mouth, leaving it slick and greasy, then positions himself between my legs.

I hear him rip open a condom wrapper. His right thumb peels my hood back and rubs my clit while his dickhead pushes through my barrier.

"Oooh… ssshhit, baby… fuck that pussy."

Sosa starts with slow, steady strokes, just enough to scrape my g-spot.

I don't know how, but not even two minutes later, I'm exploding all over his dick.

"Oh my gawd… oh my gwad… I'm cummminnnggg!"

"Look at your pussy cream all over this dick, babe… damn, your shit wetter than a motherfucker."

Squelch... squelch... squelch.

"You hear how wet your shit is?"

"Uhh-huh."

Sosa keeps stroking until I'm delirious. He spends the rest of the night fucking me silly. When my pussy gets too sore, he digs up in my ass. Each time he cums, he pulls out and floods my mouth.

"If I'm not tryna get you pregnant, my nut needs to go down your throat,"he says with finality.

As the night goes on, I'm less apprehensive and more eager to swallow his load.

By the time Sosa finally leaves, the sun's up, and I'm completely exhausted. Every hole I have is sore. It takes me a while to gather the strength to get up and wash my ass.

As I do, I can't help but smile. I hope I can lock him down; great dick and a big bag is a hard combination to find. Now that I have it, I'll do what I must to keep it.

Chapter 10

Kay

Life is definitely good. Since I've been home, Hector's been flooding me with premium coke as well as that black tar. Of course, I had to build a team to help me move it. Through Stevie and Jose, my squad's now ten deep. We're pushing dope all through Houston, and soon we'll expand to Dallas and East Texas.

They keep saying my crib's too plain, so I went furniture shopping yesterday. Tonight, I plan on finally tapping into Ms. Dean as well as Ms. T. It's not that I've been avoiding them, I've just been hella busy laying down the foundation.

Now that things are moving more fluently, I can spare a couple hours to get my dick wet. Ms. Dean's been lowkey blowing my phone up, even going as far as insinuating I was all jail talk, that I don't really intend on fucking with her like that. She's gonna be surprised when I hit her with the game plan for tonight.

I call my nigga GoDj Hefna first. He's DJ'ing at Houston's number one, premier club, *Club Legaci*. Once him and I get everything overstood, I hit Ms. Dean up.

"Hello?"

"Wassup, thunder cat?"

"Heyy, stranger. I see you finally found some time for a bitch. Now that you ain't in a cell, you act like you don't have time for ole Ms. Dean."

"It ain't even like that, Kiesha. You know I fucks with you the long way. A nigga just been going hard for that bag, is all."

"Uhh-huh... let that be the reason."

"Man, that's facts. But check game, what you got planned for tonight?"

"Nothing, this my four off right here."

"Well, put on your dancing shoes. We hittin' up Club Legaci tonight."

"Okay, now I see you. Let a bitch know she's appreciated for all the work I put in. What time you need me to be ready?"

"I'll come scoop you around ten-thirty."

"That's a bet, then. How should I dress?"

"Something tight and extra short. Oh yeah… don't wear any panties."

"Boy, your ass is up to no good."

Damn straight.

We hang up and I make my next call. After I'm done, I hit Stevie up and check the progress. Things have been going smoothly, *too* smoothly. A lot of times, when things are moving too well, you gotta watch for potholes.

After a few more calls, I'm satisfied with how shit's running, so I head upstairs to hop in the shower.

I reflect on how crazy life is. Just a year ago, I was buried in the Texas penal system. Now I'm building a powerful organization, with the help of someone I met *because* the state railroaded me.

I finish showering, wrap a towel around my waist, and head into my bedroom to get dressed.

Ding dong.

I stop dead in my tracks. *Who the hell is that?* Only a select few know where I lay my head, and I just spoke to the brothers on the phone, so it can't be them.

I head downstairs and open the door.

Imagine my surprise when I see Tianna standing there, looking like a Nubian sex goddess. Hair wrapped in a bun big as a Frisbee. Her black dress is so thin that in the right light, I can see straight through to her yellow thong.

She notices me in nothing but a towel, and her right eyebrow climbs.

"Uh, your sons ain't here," I make clear.

"I know. Can I come in?"

"Oh shit, my bad. Of course, come in."

I step aside and let her in. Her heels click-clack against the wood floors, booty cheeks dancing behind that thin material. I don't trust myself around her. I'm about to head upstairs to get dressed, but Tianna quickly sits down, crosses her legs, and gets straight to the reason she's here.

"Look, Kay… this won't take long. I'm on my way to one of my girlfriend's houses and decided to stop by so we can chat. Since you've become part of this *family,* I haven't been very hospitable. Shit, you've had this house for almost two months now, and this is the first time I've set foot in it."

I shrug, nothing else I can say or do would be appropriate.

"I'm a kept wife. My husband's gone a lot. You don't think I notice how you look at me?"

"Excuse me… the way I look at you?"

"Come on, Kay, we're both grown. Even though I have you by almost twenty years, you're still grown enough not to beat around the bush. I see the way you look at me… how your eyes drink me in. Like you're thirsting for my very essence."

Tianna uncrosses her legs, then crosses them back giving me a perfect shot of her yellow thong. *Classic Sharon Stone.*

I swallow hard. My dick starts to unfurl. I want to deny the allegations, but we both know the truth, *I want her in the worst way.*

She catches my unease and smiles slightly before continuing.

"I just want to get some things clear. My husband is a very jealous, very dangerous man. Even though he's got countless concubines, he detests the idea of me getting my rocks off with a man of my own. Now, of course, he won't lay a hand on me, I have my family and my sons to thank for that, but as for the man I'm sleeping with. That's another story."

She leans forward slightly.

"I say all that to say this, *tread lightly.* You keep sniffing around this coochie, I might just give you a taste. If nothing else, just to sample some American thug dick. But know this, this panocha comes with a warning label. It's up to you to decide if it's worth the risk."

Tianna rises, heads toward the door. Before she opens it, her eyes drop to my crotch.

"You might want to take care of that."

I glance down. My dick is at full salute, a huge tent formed beneath my towel, giving her a clear view of my glory.

"Mmh… oh my. Well, at least you answered one of my questions,"she says, closing the door behind her.

I tilt my head back, close my eyes, trying to steady my nerves. *This woman has me gone, and I haven't even laid a finger on her.* Maybe it's the danger that's so damn alluring.

I think about beating my meat, but instead, I finish getting dressed and call Ms. Dean. A couple hours later, Ms. Dean and I are circling downtown looking for parking. After twenty minutes, we finally snag a spot.

We step out looking like Hollywood celebrities. I'm draped in a baby-blue and yellow Ralph Lauren Purple Label shirt with matching shorts. Baby-blue and white Balenciaga low tops. Denver Nuggets snapback. My ice game's clean but not over the top, white gold Cuban link, white gold Cartier watch, bezel flooded with blue and yellow diamonds.

Ms. Dean didn't hold back either. Even with her state job, she blew some of her side hustle bread on a white Fendi strapless dress stopping just under her ass cheeks. White Fendi clutch. Hair pressed and shining like silk.

We walk into *Legaci* and my nigga shouts me out from the booth.

"Oh shit! If it isn't my motherfucking nigga, fresh home to the throne! The real motherfucking Snowman!"

The whole club turns. All eyes on us. Ms. Dean tightens her grip on my arm. I can tell she's loving the attention, probably never been with a nigga who moves like this.

I lead her up to the DJ booth.

"Wassup, bredren!" Hefna yells, pulling me into a brotherly hug.

"Shit, tryna get where you at," I tease. Truth is, Hefna's doing his thing, big crib in the suburbs, cocaine-white Bentley coupe, all-black Range Rover, and it's all *legit*.

He nods toward Ms. Dean. "This the one you was telling me about?"

"Yeah, that's her. She play her cards right, she might be wifey," I say boldly.

Dean lowers her head, hiding a blush. Tonight's about making her feel special. A lot of women think niggas in the pen are all talk, that once we're out, we don't really build with the women who held us down. I believe if she's sticking her neck out, risking her freedom for me, she deserves an honest shot. After we take our seats, I order a bottle of Ace of Spades and sit back, watching Hefna do his thing.

My phone vibrates: *I'm downtown.*

Kay: *I'll meet you outside.*

I turn to Dean. "I'll be right back, baby girl." She's so caught up in the vibe, she doesn't even hear me.

On my way out the club, someone familiar catches my eye. I slow my pace, making sure I'm not tripping. *It is him.*

When I was locked up, there was a nigga I kept bumping heads with named Beetle. To this day, I don't know what dude's real issue with me was, but I'm willing to bet it had something to do with Ms. Dean. Supposedly, before I hit the unit, him and her had something going. He'd been trying to get her to start dropping off, but she wasn't sure enough about him to take that risk.

Even though he couldn't prove it, he *felt* like she started coming down for me instead. That's when he started his hate campaign.

Him and I never stayed on the same section, or even the same building, so I just dismissed the nigga and kept running my bag. *I'm glad I spotted his ass first.*

I step outside and head straight to my whip. I'm not sure I can get my pole in the club, so I grab the switchblade I keep in the glove box. I don't know what type of time dude's on, but I'll be damned if I let him catch me lacking. My phone rings.

"Hello… yeah, I'm outside on the corner of Rusk and San Jacinto. Yeah, that parking lot right there… I'm standing next to a red Audi."

I hang up and wait. A few moments later, I see Ms. T's navy-blue BMW 650 turning in. Ms. Dean has no idea her homegirl will be partying with us tonight. Hopefully, by the end of the night, both of them will be stretched out in my bed.

When Ms. T hops out, I'm taken back by how good she looks out of her work uniform, red-and-white Michael Kors skirt with the matching top. Hair braided to the scalp in designs, yellow-gold loop earrings, Lady Rolex on her wrist. With those four-inch Bottega heels, Ms. T is giving Ms. Dean a run for her money.

"Heyyy, baby boy," she sings, as I wrap her in a tight hug. She smells like fresh roses.

"Damn girl, your ass is shutting shit down tonight," I compliment, giving her booty a light squeeze.

She steps back and looks me over. "Mhmm, mhmm, mhmm… you'll definitely get some of this wet-wet tonight, looking like that," she says boldly.

We start walking toward the club when an idea hits me. "I need a favor. Can you get this in for me?" I show her the knife.

She doesn't hesitate. "Boy, of course."

Ms. T opens her handbag, unzips a secret compartment, and slides the blade inside. *That's why I love a hood bitch.*

We make it to the front door. The bouncer remembers me from Hefna's earlier shout-out and lets us through with a light pat-down, doesn't even check Ms. T's bag. I have her give me the knife back before we head to the section.

As I'm walking up to VIP, I see Beetle posted near our table, trying to get Ms. Dean's attention. She doesn't look like she's feeling him. The jolly smile she had earlier is now a scowl. She sees me, and her face brightens, then drops slightly when she notices Ms. T. *Here goes nothing.*

"Hey baby, look who I found."

"Hey, Kiesha," Ms. T greets her, stepping in for a hug.

"Stacy… what you doing here?" From her tone, I can tell she's not too happy about the third wheel.

"I was supposed to meet a friend, but they canceled last minute."

Ms. T and I already agreed, no clue to Ms. Dean about the real plan until it's time to get active.

"Damn… what are the odds, Kaydon? You step outside to do something and *bump* into her,"Kiesha says, accusingly. I don't say anything. Just shrug, grab my bottle of champagne, and take a swig. The two women find their natural vibe with each other, and of course, I keep plying them with liquor to loosen them up. During one of the breaks in conversation, I introduce Ms. T to my nigga Hood Hefna. He pulls me to the side afterwards.

"Boy, I see you. So, which one you plan on tapping tonight?" he asks.

"Both," I answer, cocky.

"Okay, that's what I'm talkin' 'bout. So, what, both of them down with the action?"

"Well, not really. The bright one is, but I'm still working on the dark one," I admit.

Hefna pulls me further into the corner. "Check this out, ever heard of some shit called Demon Dust?"

I have. They were talking 'bout that shit in the pen, and Hector told me he was thinking about expanding into it. "Yeah, but I ain't never fucked with it," I tell him. He reaches in his bag, pulls out a lil' baggie with some tan-looking powder in it. Just by the eye, looks like four or five grams.

"Say, bruh, one line of this, and a bitch will fuck a whole house of niggas if you want her to."

"Man, gone on," I laugh, but his face stays dead serious.

"No cap. I've seen devoted housewives turn into dick-hungry sluts off this shit."

I grab the baggie. "Straight up?"

"Facts," he says again.

"How much?"

"They're paying up to two hundred a gram. But you can have that, welcome home, my nigga."

"'Preciate it. And don't forget, bro, don't be putting this shit on social media. I don't want anybody knowing I'm home just yet."

"Overstood. I got you."

Hefna glances at the two women dancing in their seats. "If you ever need help, or just feel like sharing with a brother, don't hesitate to call," he half-jokes. I know for a fact, being the hottest DJ in the city, spinning at the hottest club, Hefna's fucked some of the baddest women.

"Maybe we can *swap* one day," I throw back at him.

"Sure, why not."

We dab each other up, and he goes back to work. I head back over to the girls.

"Y'all want something to drink?" Ms. Dean's already lit, but Ms. T still needs to be worked on. They both say yes, so I head out of VIP toward the bar—but run across our waitress first.

"Excuse me, can you bring us another bottle of Ace, and two bottles of Ciroc?"

"Sure," she says cheerfully.

I make my way to the restroom. My bladder feels like it's about to pop. I'm standing at the urinal when I hear the bathroom door open. Don't think nothing of it, until *Thwack!* A blinding pain explodes on the right side of my face. The blow sends me reeling into the next urinal. My dick's still out, pants halfway off my ass. Before I can stand up, the toe of a boot comes rushing at my face. I turn my head just in time to absorb the blow. The boot connects anyway, I bite my tongue and white lightning clouds my brain. The bitter taste of blood floods my mouth. *Fuck!*

I've gotta shake back, quick. He comes at me again, trying to kick. This time, I grab his leg and shove him off balance. The wet floor works in my favor as he slips and stumbles back. I shake the cobwebs loose, vision clearing. That's when I see who it is. *Beetle!* I switch into savage mode, reach inside my jeans, and grab the knife hidden in my gym shorts. Lightning quick, I jab at Beetle's soft belly. Feel the resistance as the blade eats through his flesh, tearing up his insides. I hit him again, this time pushing as deep as I can.

Blood pours from the wound, around my hand, dripping down my wrist. From the look on his face, I've hit something vital. I yank the knife back. Beetle sinks down on his haunches, eyes wide in disbelief. I stand over him, disgusted. "All this behind a bitch that don't even want you," I spit. Then it hits me, *someone could walk in at any time.* I can't let them catch me like this, red handed. *Literally.* I wipe the bloody knife off on his shirt as he sits there gasping for air. After fixing myself up as best I can, I rush out the restroom and head straight for VIP. The girls see me and instantly know something's wrong.

"We gotta go. Now!"

Luckily, they don't ask any questions. Both grab their purses, and the three of us sprint out of the club.

"Just follow me," I tell Ms. T as Dean, and I hop in my whip. Pulling into traffic, I check my side and rearview mirrors. My heart's trying to claw its way out my chest.

"Fuck!" I yell, pounding my fist on the steering wheel.

Ms. Dean jumps, startled by my outburst. "Kay, what the fuck is going on? Don't have a bitch in the blind."

I glance in the rearview, Ms. T's right behind us. "Look, I can't really talk about it. Just know y'all ain't in any danger."

She looks back, spots Ms. T, then turns to me. "Speaking of *y'all*, what you got going on with Stacy? Y'all fucking?"

She's choosing right now to get on some insecure shit.

I give it to her raw. "Not yet, but I plan on it."

She jerks back like I slapped her. "What does that mean?"

"It means by the end of the night, I'm tryna fuck both of y'all."

Her mouth drops in shock before she turns away, staring out the window. She stays quiet for about five minutes. Then, almost in a whisper, "Afterwards… what does that mean for me and you?"

"What you mean? Don't shit change. I'm fucking with you the long way. This ain't about feelings, it's about fun. We still gone be us," I say, placing my hand on her thigh to reassure her.

"Okay," she answers, just as we pull into the parking lot of Hotel Derek off 6-10 and 59.

At the counter, I pay for the room while the girls stand to the side, awkward, neither willing tobreak the silence. We head up to the Presidential Suite. The second we walk in, I know it's 'bout to be a hell of a night. King-size bed with red satin sheets. Black carpet thick and plush. Floor-to-ceiling windows showing off a lit-up skyline. I pull the curtains open to let the moonlight flood in.

"The lady at the desk said this suite has two bathrooms. Y'all can go ahead and shower first."

They glance at each other, then head to separate bathrooms. I hit the mini bar, pour a shot of Cognac, and remember the pack of Demon Dust Hefna gave me at the club. I dig it out my pocket and pour the contents on the counter. The powder's got a brownish hue with sparkling crystals. If I didn't know better, I'd think it was candy. I pull a hundred-dollar bill, roll it into a tube, and snort a line. The sensation's indescribable, like getting kicked in the face by a horse, except instead of pain, I'm in pure bliss. My dick's rockin' up, but pussy ain't even on my mind. My brain's a kaleidoscope of colors. My whole body's tingling. Every nerve is vibrating. I strip down to my Perry Ellis boxers and stumble out to the balcony for fresh air.

This shit is a wonder drug. I need to convince Hector to get his hands on some. What feels like seconds, probably ten, fifteen minutes, Ms. T comes out the bathroom wrapped in a towel, dripping wet. Just seeing her like that has my dick hard as doing life without parole.

"Boy, what's wrong with your eyes? Your pupils look like two pennies," she says.

I wet my lips. "Come here. I wanna give you something."

She follows me back inside. I hand her the rolled-up bill. "Try this out."

She hesitates. "What's this, Kay? I don't fuck with no dog food."

Even though I don't actually *know* what this is, I make it seem like I do.

"Girl, this ain't no boy. This some new shit called Demon Dust. Trust me, you'll love it."

It don't take much prodding for Ms. T to grab the tube, bend over, and snort a fat-ass line through her left nostril. She tilts her head back, expecting a slow drain, but what she gets is a full-on kick to her senses. She buckles, staggers back onto the sofa, and collapses, legs falling wide open, her pretty pink pussy popping right at me. I freeze, transfixed, watching her pussy pulse like it's alive. Like it's breathing.

Or better yet, like a heartbeat. Her lips are engorged, slick, and meaty looking. Ms. T jerks, and a thick rivulet of cum pours out of her. My dick's standing straight up, feeling like it's about to buss, like an overcooked Ballpark Frank. I pull my boxers all the way off and take two steps.

"What the fuck? That's how y'all do the game? I thought we was doing this together."

Ms. Dean catches me with my dick in my hands. *Literally.* I turn toward her, piece in hand, as I approach. "We are, baby. Look, I want you to try something for me." I walk her over to the pile of dope.

"Kay, what the fuck is this? You know I don't do drugs."

"I know, baby, but this is a one-time thing. Me and Stacy already on our level." I know once I mention Stacy doing it, she'll feel pressured. Nobody wants to get outdone by the competition.

Ms. Dean leans down and vacuums up a nice-sized line. As the drug bulldozes through her system, I decide to hop in the shower. Ten minutes later, I step out to find Ms. Dean on her hands and knees while Ms. T's got her booty cheeks spread, licking around the rim of her asshole. I don't wait for no formal invite. I get behind Ms. T and slide my middle finger up and down her crack. *Damn, a nigga might need a water slide for her shit.* I grab my piece, line myself up, and with one great push, bury my dick inside her, balls deep.

The rest of the night is one for the books. The way they go at it, you'd swear they been fucking for years. Nothing's off-limits. At one point, I got them side by side, fucking Ms. Dean in her ass for twenty, thirty strokes, then switching to Ms. T's ass for twenty, thirty more. Only thing I don't do is nut in their pussies. *I can't afford no kids right now.*

We go until eleven in the morning, all tapped out. After a shower, I hug Ms. T goodbye, give her a long, wet kiss. Her sex game was exactly what I expected. *I know for a fact I'll be running up in her on the regular.*

On the ride to drop Ms. Dean off, I can tell she's got regrets. She had a front-row seat to how Ms. T put that pussy on me, and now she's probably thinking she'll get replaced. But nothing could be further from the truth. As long as she ain't tripping on me fucking her homegirl, we won't have problems. I drop her off, hug and kiss her too, just to make sure she knows things are the same.

On the way home, a text from Hector hits my phone:*Hector: Chucho's back.* Time to pay my dues.

Demon

"Demon, I won't be back until tonight. You want me to pick something up, or you gonna order DoorDash?"

Keeda's getting ready to head out for work. Her uniform pants so tight, her camel toe's popping, looking like a baseball between her legs. I wanna say something, but I ain't trying to come off like no jealous ass sucka nigga.

It's been three weeks since I moved in, and shit's going great. I can't fuck it up. I had no idea she was such a boss freak. She *loves* to eat dick, and I better not try to pull out, she wants all a nigga's nut like a greedy-ass squirrel. Don't get it twisted, though. I ain't come empty-handed. I slid her a rack when I pulled up to help with the bills, even though she insisted I didn't have to.

One thing my sister taught me, a woman won't respect you if you ain't an earner.

"Naw baby, I'll order something to eat. You ain't gotta do all that."

She walks over and gives me a deep, sensual kiss. I taste her cherry lip gloss as I slide my hand between her thighs, cupping that fat cat.

"Boy, you better quit. You know once my engine start running, I don't stop 'til I run outta gas."

You ain't never lied. I reluctantly let her go and watch Keeda walk out the door for work.

Thirty minutes later, I'm walking around the apartments on my way to kick it with my nigga Manny. He'd just moved into the jets a week after I did. We met one day when he was looking for some Loud. Once I found out he'd just moved in, we clicked, kindred spirits.

He's originally from Florida but moved out here running from the laws. I can tell bro's a killa. *It takes one to know one.* When I pull up to his spot, I'm surprised to see two other niggas already posted in his living room.

"*Demon Time*, wassup,"Manny calls out, standing up to give me a half hug.

"Same ole shit, what's good?"

"Shit, we putting a lil play together. Oh, let me introduce you."

He points to the darker of the two, a short, heavyset nigga with beady eyes and a pug nose. "This is Lil Rob. He stays over here by the Washingteria."

I nod his way.

"This his kinfolk, Tiger. He's from Sunnyside." Tiger's about my height, red-skinned with bad acne.

I don't shake either of their hands, but I sit to hear what Manny's cooking.

"Rob got a play for us to hit. It's a mom-and-pop store. They only deposit to the bank once a month. On average, every deposit is 'bout a hundred-fifty to two-fifty bands. According to Rob, they are using the business to wash dirty money."

"Okay, so how we getting the bag? I've done more kick doors than I can count, but never a commercial burglary. I know niggas who have, and they always say the same thing, do your homework. Sometimes you hit six figures, sometimes you crap out. I ain't tryna do no dry runs,"I tell the group. Rob breaks it all down, how we'd use walkie-talkies to communicate, the blow torch and sledgehammer for entry, even the alarm system and how we'd get around it. After grilling him with questions, I felt confident he knew what he was talking about. We agree to meet up around nine. The spot is about two hours away, and we wanna be out there no later than midnight so we can scope it and *go in* between *1:30–2:30 a.m.*

As soon as they leave, I turn to Manny. "How you know these niggas? You trust 'em?"

"Well, I won't say I trust 'em. I just know when it comes to *going in*, they know their shit. They been doing this for years, all over the country."

"Aight. Well, if them niggas get on some weird shit, Imma park they ass," I state.

"Agreed."

Manny and I spend the next couple hours blowing on some Za, getting mentally right. When nine o'clock comes, Rob and Tiger pull back up dressed in all black. We head outside and follow them to a navy-blue Ford Explorer parked sideways.

"Who's shit is this?" I ask, catching a whiff of stale crack smoke as I hop in the backseat.

"This lil smoker bitch named Paula. We got it for three days," Tiger tells us.

I pull my Glock 32 and set it in my lap. Even though this is a burglary and technically I shouldn't need it, ain't no way I'm going on a lick with niggas I don't know without my pole. Manny sees me, smirks, and does the same.

I nod his way. *We're agreed, if either one of these niggas get on some dumb shit, we popping their tops.* We head out. Two hours and fifteen minutes later, we pull into a small town. Just as we hit the city limits, my phone vibrates.

Keeda: *R U aight***Demon:** *Yeah. On bidness. Will B Back 2morrow.*

Keeda: *B careful baby***Demon:** *Got U*

I turn my phone off. Rob said to leave our phones, something about if the play went wrong, they could track us through the cell towers. *Fuck all that.* I need to be able to reach out if things get ugly. We turn onto a four-lane road.

Streets are damn near deserted. We pass a big building on the corner of the intersection.

"That's the building right there," Rob points out. "We gonna park two blocks over and walk."

I slip on my gloves, my ski mask/beanie, and slide my Glock into the small of my back before grabbing my tools. Rob finds a spot to park, tucked away from the main road. Each one of us got our assignment. Rob cuts the alarm, and we rush in. I can hear Tiger on the walkie giving updates on how the streets are looking, while Manny goes to work on the safe with the blow torch. Not even ten minutes later, he's burned a hole the size of a football. I shove my hand in and start stuffing an all-black, king-size pillowcase with cash.

"Say y'all, twelves on the way down there."

I yank the last stack out, and the three of us rush out the back. At the same time, Tiger's hopping into the Explorer, headed to meet us at the rendezvous. Everything's smooth, until we hit a side street and see patrol cars coming our way.

"Shit!" I yell, busting a left with Rob while Manny breaks right.

I toss the pillowcase over a fence, then hop it. Rob lands next to me with a thud. Blue and red lights flash off the windows as patrol units circle. It's been a long time since I ran from the cops. Sweat's pouring down my face, my black tee clinging to my chest.

"Look, bruh, we should stash the money 'til it's safe. That way if the laws run down on us, they ain't got no evidence," Rob says.

I hate parting with my bread once it's in my hands, but it makes sense. "Aight, but where?"

We scan for a spot. I see one, about ten yards away, there's an old, abandoned building with a gap in its foundation. Pretty sure I can squeeze the bread in there. I tell Rob, and we take off toward it. I check the hole, deep enough. Perfect. I grab the pillowcase and start sliding it inside. I feel Rob's presence behind me. At first, I think nothing of it. Then, a sudden chill creeps over me. The hairs on my neck stand up.

As a killa myself, I got a sixth sense when deaths is in the air. My Glock's in the small of my back, but before I can reach it—

Psssft. Psssft.

Two muffled shots.

I dive to the side, reaching for my pole. What I see stops me cold, Manny, standing with his Sig out, suppressor on the end. Rob's face down, a hole in the back of his head so big I can see his brains, mangled and mushy. My eyes snap to Manny, looking for an explanation. He nods toward the ground, a few feet from Rob. I follow his line of sight. *I see it.* A black Smith & Wesson, two feet from Rob's outstretched arm.

"He was about to blow your shit off, bruh," Manny says. "I'm glad I pulled up when I did."

My heart skips. *Damn… I was slipping.* If Manny didn't show up, I'd be the one laid out, brains watering the grass.

"Where y'all niggas at? Rob… Manny… Y'all there?" Tiger's voice crackles through the walkie.

Manny and I lock eyes. We both thinking the same thing, *Tiger's gotta go.*

No doubt, he was in on whatever Rob had lined up for me. Manny grabs the walkie.

"Wassup, Tiger? Twelves all over this bitch. We had to split up. I don't know where Rob or D's at, but I'm coming back around to meet you on the street before we get to the spot."

"Bet, meet me behind the doctor's office."

"Fa' sho."

Manny cuts his eyes at me. "Check it… we gon' have to spank his ass and leave him here. He's expecting me, but—"

"I got him," I cut in, eager. Just knowing his boy tried to end my life got me seeing blood.

Manny and I put a quick plan together. I follow at a distance while he makes his way toward the doctor's office. Tiger pulls in, parks, and cuts off his headlights. I watch Manny cross the street and start talking to him. I circle wide, creeping up from behind. As I get close, I hear Tiger ask,

"Who got the money?"

"I don't know. Last I saw, it was Rob."

Tiger's face twists, like he's worried Rob might run off with the bread.

I move in slow. Tiger must catch the change in Manny's eyes, 'cause he stops mid-sentence and starts to turn. I swing my pistol,

Thwack!

Steel cracks against his dome. He stumbles into the Explorer's door, leaving a deep dent.

Before he can recover, I pounce. Barrel pressed to his sternum to muffle the sound—

Thucka. Thucka. Thucka.

Three quick pops. Tiger's body jerks with each shot ripping through him, blowing out his back. Dead in seconds.

"Let's get the fuck up outta here," Manny urges.

I snatch the bag of money. We hop in the Explorer and burn it back to Houston. When we get back, we head to Keeda's crib to count it up. I unlock the door and walk in to see her laid out on the couch, skimpy satin panties, baby tee, sleeping on her stomach. Panties jacked up in her crack, one cheek hanging out.

"Damn," Manny mutters behind me.

I shake her awake. She blinks up at me, surprised. "Heyyy baby, you're home. What time, oh shit!" She spots Manny and tries to cover up, but the blanket's already on the floor.

"Damon, why you ain't tell me you was bringing company?"

"It wasn't planned. We need to handle some bidness real quick. Give me a few minutes and I'll be in bed."

She gets up, ass cheeks jiggling, her toned body on full display. I know Manny's catching the show. I ain't tripping, bro saved my life. Hell, truth be told, if he wanted to fuck my bitch, I might let him. Once we're in the bedroom, I dump the money onto the coffee table. It takes forty-nine minutes to count, $230,000. We split it down the middle. I see Manny to the door, then hop in the shower. While the water's running, I'm already thinking about what to do with my cut. When I moved in with Keeda, I took the car back to my sister. *Tomorrow, I'm copping a whip.* Nothing flashy, maybe a Tahoe. I'll slide Keeda fifteen bands to do her thing and stash the rest for a rainy day.

Fresh out the shower, I slide into bed naked. She stirs when she feels me next to her. Spoon position turns into my dick rockin' up. I pull her panties to the side and slide into that oven-hot, gushy, wet-ass pussy.

Perfect end to a lucrative night. After I bust all up in her, I'm out like a newborn.

Chapter 11

Claudia

This is my second time dealing with my boss, Lance. I'm not as nervous as before, this time, I know what to expect. Still, the anxiety's there. I just hate I had to lie to Harrell. Again. He's so trusting, never once questioning me. I tell him where I'm *supposedly* going, what I'm *supposedly* doing, and he just accepts it. That blind trust? Makes me feel even worse.

I pull into the affluent neighborhood once again and check the time the appointment is set for. *9:23 p.m.* I can't be a minute late, or a minute early, for that matter. I park in front of the two-story brick home and wait for the clock to strike *9:22* before I step out. Today, I'm wearing an easily accessible plaid skirt, a white dress shirt, and all-white cotton panties. *Classic Catholic school girl look.* My four-inch stiletto heels click-clack against the pavement as I make my way toward the front door. *Knock, knock, knock.*

Seconds later, the door swings open. Lance is standing there in his usual attire, black slacks, black dress shirt completely unbuttoned, and once again, barefoot. What he has in his hand makes me pause. Lance is holding a leash attached to a dog collar. My heart skips a beat. So does my clit. He steps to the side and allows me entry. I take three timid steps forward, then stop. He whispers in my ear, *"On your knees."*

Without hesitation, I drop, feeling the cool tile against my shins and kneecaps. I keep my head down until he commands me to lift it. Lance pulls my long, luxurious hair away from my neckline before tying it up with a scrunchie.

Suddenly, the leather collar wraps around my neck and tightens. "Today, you are my bitch in heat. You're going to be a good little doggie, aren't you?" I nod. Lance pats me on the head. "Good girl." Then, he clicks his tongue twice and takes off walking.

The leash is about four feet long, but I don't wait for the slack to tighten. I make sure to keep pace. Once again, he has guests in the house. My head's down, so I can't see them, but based on the voices, I can tell there's at least six or seven of them.

"Ladies and gentlemen, our favorite pet has arrived. She's in heat, so you'll have to be careful. She'll fuck anything in her vicinity." Light chuckles come from the group.

Lance walks me out of the living room and chains me to a table in the hallway. One of the guest bathrooms is directly in front of me. It doesn't take long for my first visitor to arrive. I sit on my haunches and watch him enter the bathroom to take a piss. After he's done, he walks over and offers me his cock to suck. I taste the sourness of his urine on my tongue, but it's not enough to make me gag. His dick isn't very long, but it has some girth to it, so it easily clogs my airways. *Awka, awka, awka, awka.*

He fucks my throat savagely until his dick jerks and cock snot fills my mouth. I swallow him down with a loud, satisfied moan. After he wipes his dickhead off on my face, he tucks himself back in his pants, pats me on the head, and says, "That's a good girl." My cotton panties are already a soiled mess.

The next one is a tall, older man with a gray beard and bald head. He, too, enters the restroom and starts pissing. "Oh shit, I must be drunk as hell," he says. "I've pissed all over the toilet seat. Come here, girl."

I crawl into the restroom. He grabs me by my ponytail and sticks my nose into the waste. "Bad girl. Clean that up." I hesitate only a fraction of a second, close my eyes, and begin to lick up his piss. "Good girl, good girl," he coos, patting my head.

Once the rim's clean, he pulls his dick out, and I begin to lick under his nut sack. My tongue snakes behind his balls, trying to wiggle its way through his ass crack. He grabs me by my hair and yanks me upward, feeding me his hardened dick. It isn't big, so I'm able to devour him whole. Moments later, his gooey goodness squirts into my mouth.

I'm thinking the rest of the night will be more of the same, but instead, Lance comes to retrieve me. My panties are sticking to my pussy lips. I can smell the cum and piss on my breath. He walks me into a back room filled with all types of sex gadgets. There's a table-like structure in the center of the room. My heart quickens when I spot it. Something tells me this table, and I are about to get real acquainted. Lance orders me to *"stay"* as he fiddles with the table. I watch him pull on levers and knobs until it folds in on itself, forming a ninety-degree angle. With two clicks of his tongue, he motions for me to get on it. My stomach flat, ass up, I'm strapped in. Just in case that isn't enough, he ties my legs to a metal bar that's attached to a separate device.

"My friends told me how you made a mess, pissing all over the place. You've been a very bad dog."

He grabs a thick, wide paddle. I quiver, teeth chattering, juices pouring down the back of my legs.

"So, I will have to discipline you, so that you will be potty trained,"Lance says, finishing up the straps. Slowly, he walks behind me, but because of my position, I lose sight of him. Suddenly, without warning, my panties are jerked and ripped in half. The cloth cuts into my pussy crack, my thick, meaty sex lips hanging out on each side.

Lance runs his fingers up and down my slit. He sniffs, *no doubt smelling my odor off his fingers.*

"Is this piss I smell?"

I want to answer, *"No, it's cum,"*but I dare not speak. Suddenly, he comes across my booty with the paddle.

"Uggghhh," I moan, almost tearfully.

"You will learn to behave yourself and not piss on the floor." *WHAP!*

"Mmmmhm," I cry out in muffled silence. My ass cheeks feel like they're on fire. *WHAP! WHAP! WHAP!* He keeps throttling me until my eyes are wet with tears. But so is my chocha. I want to rub my pussy so bad it's driving me insane.

With each smack, the paddle connects with my cheeks and my cunt. I've already came twice, and now my clit feels like it's about to explode.

Lance rubs my booty with something cool and slick. It's soothing, but foreboding.

"You took your spanking very well, my pet. I know how much you're in heat, so I'll give you a little treat."

He begins rubbing the unknown substance between my cheeks, up and down my crack. I feel pressure at my opening, his fingers penetrating my back door. I flinch but accept his intrusion. First one, then a second finger finds its way inside. Lance slowly but forcefully fingers my asshole, opening me up.

"Yesss, that's it. Open up for me, my little pet."

With my face down and my ass tooted up, I'm at his complete mercy.

"What do we have here?" another male voice says, stepping into the room. I can tell he's not one of the ones I serviced earlier.

"Just getting ready to go. What do you think?" Lance asks him.

"Mmhm. I would need a more *in-depth* look. But she seems ready."

"Well, give her a spin," Lance tells him, like I'm a four-wheeler on an old country road.

The visitor unbuckles his pants. I hear a condom wrapper rip. I brace myself. Not being able to see what's going on is nerve-racking and erotic at the same time.

The tip of his cock rests at the entrance of my back door. Slowly, he pushes through, and after a soft *pop*, his dickhead's buried in my shithole. Even though I can't see it, it feels wide as hell as he opens me all the way. I bite my lip as our new guest saws into my anal cavity. If I think he's going to be gentle, I'm sadly mistaken. He fucks me like I'm an ex-wife who took half his bank account. When he finally nuts, I don't know if it's blood or cum seeping down the backs of my thighs. Lance doesn't give me time to check. Someone else enters the room and slides himself into my asshole, balls deep.

For the rest of the night, I'm anally abused until the last man is tired and heads home. I lay there, propped on the table, asshole gaped open. I can literally feel the cool air circulating inside it. Finally, Lance unstraps me, and I gingerly head outside to my car. It takes me five minutes just to sit down in the seat. *I'm so glad I didn't eat anything after I took a shit this morning.* Now *that* would have been embarrassing. I crank the car up, head to a motel room to get clean and change. I hope Harrell's too tired to want sex. If he does, at least my pussy's been virtually untouched all evening.

AD

I park down the street and kill the engine. The clock on the dash reads *1:37 a.m.* Usually around this time, the trap isn't as busy. A lot of the custo's are out clubbing and won't be back until three in the morning.

I've been scoping these two young niggas out for the past week. They specialize in exotic weed and pills. I don't know exactly how much bread they have in there, but one night I counted forty-two custos in two hours. If you multiply that by twenty, that's eight hundred and forty dollars. Shit, at that rate, they should be clearing two to three bands a day. I'm not really looking for a life-changing lick, I'm just trying to come up on some bread, period.

Hiding out at Tink's, I haven't been able to stop messing with that shit. It's like it helps me focus a lot better. I grab my pole and double-check to make sure it's fully loaded before I hop out. The door to the garage opens, and one of the young nigga's heads outside to his car. I duck down, praying he doesn't notice me in the shadows. He doesn't and keeps on pushing until he's out the neighborhood. *This is my chance.*

With only one nigga in the spot, this shit's damn near automatic. I wipe my nose with the back of my hand and speed-walk toward the trap. *Knock, knock, knock.* The lil nigga opens the door, sees me, and lets me in. I've been purposely shopping with them all week. To them, I'm just another regular.

"What you need, same thing?" he asks.

"Uhh, yeah. Just give me an eighth of Loud and ten X-pills."

As he turns around to grab my order, I pull my pole out and smack him in the back of the head. *Thwack! Thump, thump.* He falls onto the coffee table, breaking it into pieces. Before he can recover, I'm on him, pistol to his chin.

"Where's the money at, nigga?"

"We ain't got no money. Lil Harvey just took it with him," he tells me.

What? Can't be. I didn't see him with nothing in his hands.

"Lil nigga, you're lying. I'm not the one to play games with. Just give me the money, and I won't kill you."

The lil nigga tightens his mouth up, trying to play tough. I smack his front teeth out with the pistol.

"Agghhh,"he hollers, mouth full of jagged, bloody teeth.

"You still wanna play tough? Where's the fucking money at?"

He squeezes his eyes shut like he's bracing for another hit. When it doesn't come, he opens them back up. I've got the pistol pointed right between his eyes.

"Either you tell me where the bread's at, or I blow your shit out the back of your skull. Then, I'll go look for it myself."

He starts trembling in fear. Suddenly, something catches his attention, his eyes dart behind me. Relief washes over his face. The cocaine heightens my intuition. I quickly raise my right arm just as a leg tries to connect with the side of my head. A pound of pain shoots through my arm, making me drop my pistol. I growl in agony. *My shit might be broke... or at least fractured.*

I try to reach for the gun with my left, but whoever's behind me starts pummeling me with their fists. The blows aren't heavy, but them bitches still hurt. I shield myself as best I can until I can turn around and get better positioning. When I do, I see the nigga behind me is a *female.* I guess one of these niggas decided to call a lady friend over. I let her get a few more shots in so I can get closer. Then, with one fluid motion, I dip and scoop her ass up. *Bam!* I slam her onto the couch, tilting it over. White-hot pain shoots through my forearm. Now that I'm face-to-face with her, I can tell she's probably barely out of high school. I head-butt her a few good times. Her nose breaks, and she's out like a light. I turn around to reach for my gun, only to see the lil nigga has my shit aimed and ready to shoot. My instincts kick in. I dodge left just as he lets one go. *Bocka!*

Shit! I gotta get out of here.

I run toward the back room as he fires wildly. *Bocka! Bocka!* Two slugs penetrate the wall, chewing it up. With no legitimate weapon, the only logical option is retreat.

I see a window, quickly open it, dive through, and run back to my car. As soon as I get in, I crank the engine and hightail it out the neighborhood. My heart's galloping in my chest. I'm soaking wet, drenched in sweat. My left arm's throbbing something serious.

I don't even make it all the way back to Tink's before pulling over and digging out the powder pack. To be honest,

I'm glad I was high, because of the coke, I was able to maneuver and dodge a fatal incident. I bump the last two hits, relax, and let the coke drain. Once that oh-so-familiar numb, warm, fuzzy feeling sets in, I put the car in drive and head on home.

When I get back to Tink's, she's up watching *Law & Order*. I absolutely hate that show, but since I don't have shit else to do, I take a quick shower and join her in the living room.

She's got on a green-and-purple robe with flower prints, hair wrapped up in a red bandanna. I can tell that underneath her robe, it's nothing but bra and panties. Even though Tink smokes, she still has sex appeal. She's not as fine as she used to be, plus she's missing her top row of teeth, but she's better looking than the majority of women who've been smoking crack for the last twenty-plus years.

As I sit on the couch, I wince and grab my arm. It doesn't go unnoticed.

"Boy, what's wrong with you?"

"I fucked my arm up. I don't know if it's broken, but that motherfucka hurts like hell."

She gets off the recliner, flips the light on, and takes a look. My arm's bruised and swollen, but she makes me open and close my fist.

"It's not broken," she says. Tink heads to the freezer, comes back with a bag of ice. "Keep that on there."

Then she disappears into the bedroom and returns with a couple Percs. *Thank God.* I pop both, then sit back and wait on the drug to take effect. Once the Percs do their thing, that familiar itch returns. With no supply, I'm beginning to fiend. Tink reclines in her chair, locked into her show, but I can tell she's starting to *jones* too. Finally, she gets up and heads to her room to smoke one. After she closes the door, I sit there contemplating. *Don't do it, nigga. That powder's already bad. If you fuck with that, you'll be all the way outta there.*

Then there's another part of me saying, *Fuck all that. I'm on the run for murder. My baby momma's snitching on me, so unless I pop her, I'll be gone for life. So what if I do it? No one will know except for Tink, and she's gon' fuck with me regardless.*

I get off the couch and make my way to Tink's bedroom. Without knocking, I push the door open. She's sitting Indian style on the bed with the pipe in her mouth, about to light it. Her coochie's popping out, lips hanging from the seams of her panties. She sees me and tries to hide the pipe, *as if I didn't know she smoked.*

"What you doing in here, AD? You need something?"

"Uh, you can say that. I'm tryna see if a nigga can smoke one with you?"

Tink looks at me confused. "I ain't got no more weed right now. I only got—"

"I know what you got."

She stares through me, like she doesn't even recognize the nigga standing in front of her. After a long, awkward moment, she holds out the pipe and lighter. I walk toward her in a zombie-like state, unbelieving I'm about to do what I'm about to do. I sit next to her on the bed, put the pipe to my lips, and light it.

Once I pull the first toke in, my ears pop and start ringing. My senses are heightened; it's like cocaine times five. I blow the smoke out and ride the wave. My lips feel dry; I can't stop licking them. I pass the pipe to Tink, and she does her thing. I close my eyes and enjoy the roller coaster. Suddenly, I feel a pair of hands tugging at my belt buckle. I look down and see Tink trying to unbutton my shorts. I stare at her questioningly.

"I just wanna taste it real quick. Sharday told me your dick tastes *soooo* good. I just want a quick taste," she practically begs.

I've been knowing Tink for so long, I always looked at her like an aunt. But truth be told, she ain't my aunt, and right now, the way I'm feeling, she can get it. I help her get my shorts off, and before I know it, her lips are wrapped around my dick. The first thing I notice is how smooth her gums feel on the head of my cock. I don't know if it's the dope or what, but her mouth feels extra wet. Her saliva's dripping all over my balls and down the crack of my ass. She bites down with the top of her mouth and gums my dickhead.

Over the next few hours, I fuck Tink like she's, my wife. I even eat out her ass and pussy, nothing's off limits. When morning comes, we realize we're out of dope.

"Don't worry, baby. I'll have some more for us when I come back home tonight," she assures me as we're lying in bed, sweaty, smelling like dick, pussy, and ass.

Now that I'm coming down from the binge, I feel shitty as hell. I can't believe I'm smoking crack and laid up with a certified dopefiend. *Damn, a nigga's down bad.* I gotta shake this shit, but I can't shake it until I shake the murder charge. Only way to do that is to make sure the witness is dead.

Andrea has to go. And soon!

Chapter 12

Andrea

"Girl, where the hell is we at? This don't look like Westheimer," I ask Mary as we cruise in her car.

"That's 'cause it ain't. I need to holler at my brother Emmanuel real quick," she says as we drive through Pasadena, aka Stankadena.

Her and I have been going strong for a couple months now. This is the first time she's taken me to see her big brother. From what she's told me; he's not someone to be played with—supposedly a high-ranking member of the Mexican Mafia. I know Mary looks up to him, and even though she won't admit it, what he has to say about me is important to her.

"Aww shit, I'm not tryna get my head chopped off, Mary," I tease.

"Whatever, Drea. My brother's really a big-ass teddy bear."

"Yeah, maybe with you. You his baby sister, he 'sposed to be."

We pull up to a single-story brick home off a street next to Red Bluff. No expensive cars outside, no people hanging around. Honestly, it doesn't even look like anyone lives here. We hop out, and Mary walks straight in like she owns the place. Of course, I follow her lead.

We step into the living room and immediately realize we've made a mistake. Four white bricks of cocaine sit on the table. Mary looks at me when she realizes our fuck-up, but before we can backpedal out the house, Emmanuel emerges from the back room. He's shirtless, covered in prison ink, even his hands are tatted, with a picture of a rosary. About five foot ten, a hundred eighty-five pounds, not as big as I imagined, but the look he gives Mary and me puts fear in me just the same.

"Marisol, what the fuck? Who the hell is this?"

Mary throws up her hands in defense. "My bad, E. I didn't know. I should've called. I just wanted to stop by and say hi. This is my girl, Andrea. She's cool, she won't say shit."

He looks at her like she's remedial. "Everybody says they won't say shit… until they run their mouths."

Mary puts her head down. She can't rebuttal that. Emmanuel sees how embarrassed he's made his little sister and tries a different approach.

"Mary, I love you, and I'm glad you came by. But next time, please knock or call first."

"Si, brother. I apologize."

Emmanuel gives her a hug, then turns his attention to me.

"So, you're Andrea? Well, my sister obviously likes you a lot if she brought you to my house. I wish we would've met in better circumstances, but it is what it is. I hope you practice discretion. Please, for my sake… and yours, don't tell no one what you've seen here today."

"Trust me, I won't say shit. I've seen worse than this and didn't snitch or run my mouth about it. I'm from the streets; I know the code by heart."

He smiles at that. "Okay, well… where are you ladies headed?"

We spend the next thirty minutes kicking it with Emmanuel. When he finds out we're heading to the Galleria, he peels Mary off a couple bands to go shopping with. He's so generous, he gives me a band too. I think it's sort of like hush money, though. *Oh well!*

We pull into the Galleria about forty minutes after leaving Emmanuel's crib. After we valet the car, we walk in like we own the place. Honestly, our little couple of bands ain't shit in a spot like this, but try telling us that. Regardless of how much money we have in our pockets, we're still a couple of bad bitches.

"Where you wanna hit up first?"

"How 'bout Coach,"I suggest.

We both buy a pair of patent leather sneakers that cost three-fifty a piece. Afterwards, we head over to the Ed Hardy store. As I'm walking, someone catches my eye, a dark-skinned brother, dressed in a blue-and-white True Religion outfit with an Indianapolis Colts snapback. His neck and wrist are shimmering. I search his face for recognition. Then it hits me.

Willie G... and he's looking fine as fuck!

I stutter-step and damn near make a beeline toward him. Willie G's a hustler with long paper and an even longer dick. I met him one night partying at Club Heat. I ended up going home with him, eating on his dick the whole way there. After he realigned my insides, I was hooked. We messed around strong for about seven months, until he caught a federal pistol case and had to do thirty-two months. I'm too much of a busybody to sit still and hold a nigga down while he's in jail, so we lost touch.

As soon as I see him, my pussy starts to purr. *She remembers the beatdowns he used to put on her. And just like me, she likes it rough.* I have to check myself before Mary catches me eyeing dude. Since her and I have gotten serious, I haven't so much as smelled a piece of dick—until now.

I've been cool, but seeing *Big Dick Willie* has me going through withdrawals. I silently *will* him to look my way. He's with one of his boys, deep in conversation, but I know it ain't as important as what I got in store for him.

"What do you think about these?" Mary asks, breaking me out of my reverie.

"Huh? Oh... they're straight,"I respond dryly.

I eye Willie over her shoulder and, bingo, he spots me. Slowly at first, like his brain is playing catch-up with his eyes. Then he snaps his head, taps his homeboy, and heads my way.

Shit, shit, shit. I wasn't expecting this.

As Mary babbles on about different color schemes, Willie's closing the gap between us. I pick up a shirt and top before locking eyes with him, subtly shaking my head. *No.* Luckily, he picks up on it and stops dead in his tracks. I dart my eyes toward Mary, letting him know, *not in front of her.*

He looks around for a safe spot to meet, then eyes the dressing room. He smiles and heads that way. I wait about two minutes before making my move.

"I'll be right back, I'm 'bout to go try this on real quick,"I tell her.

She looks up, smiles, and goes back to bargain shopping. As soon as I step into the dressing room, Willie grabs two handfuls of my ass, sucking and biting on my earlobe. He knows that's my spot. I grab his piece, squeezing it through the thick denim jeans.

That bad boy grows at a rapid rate, and before I know it, the head's popping out from behind his belt buckle. Pre-cum oozes from the tip. I smear it off with my fingers, then suck them clean. Willie's breathing heavy.

"Damn, Drea… a nigga needs some of that wet right now. It ain't gon' take long,"he begs.

Even though I want to more than anything, my more rational mind wins out.

"Not right now. Give me your number, and I'll hit you tonight so we can link up."

"Pshht, don't do the game like that. A nigga ain't seen you in three years, at least top me off real quick."

Willie unbuckles his belt, unzips, and out comes his massive cock. I watch him stroke that boy, and my mouth waters. My chest starts heaving. I bend over at the waist and take him in my mouth. Right here in the Ed Hardy dressing room, while my girlfriend's walking around the store, I let

Willie fuck my mouth until he jerks and unloads a quart of cum down my throat. I swallow every delicious drop.

"Aggghh… ssshit, girl. I see you still got it," he huffs as I pull the last remnants from his nut sack.

Once he's emptied, I let his dick fall, stand up, and fix myself in the full-length mirror.

"Look, let me leave first. Wait about two minutes before you come out," I tell him.

"Who's ole girl? I know that ain't your girlfriend. You love dick too much to play strictly for the other team."

I don't respond to that. Instead, I say, "I'll call you tonight," as I walk out the dressing room.

I find Mary checking out a pair of Ed Hardy tights. I'm careful not to get too close, *I don't want her to smell dick on my breath.*

She turns to me, holding up a pair of black-and-red tights. "Do you like these?"

I nod. "They're perfect."

She heads to the counter to pay for them as I steer toward the entrance. Willie comes out of the dressing room with a smug look on his face. He leaves, but not before making sure to palm my ass as he passes by. I quickly turn toward Mary, hoping she didn't notice. Luckily, her focus is on the cashier. I mug Willie but can't help being turned on by his brazen behavior.

Willie turns the corner, and Mary meets me at the store's entrance, bags in hand. I can't help but think to myself, *Now I know how vegetarians feel when they see a slab of baby back ribs. Only difference is, I gotta have mine.*

Kelsey

"What do you want?"

"Umm, get me a number five with bacon and extra cheese," I tell Tori B as we're parked in the drive-thru.

The next day after I let it *slip* where I work, Tori was up there looking for me, *like I knew he would.* After a couple conversations, we were at the room getting our freak on. To be completely honest, the dick wasn't as good as I thought it would be.

I don't know if he realizes it or not, but I been handling black cock since high school. A motherfucker has to come on with it. I only came once, and even the late, great Reverend Cooper made sure I got at least two every time we had sex, *and he was pushing fifty years old.*

After we grab our food, I try to finesse some info out of him.

"Tori, how long you been on the East?"

"Shit, damn near my whole life. My people moved here from San Antonio when I was a lil' baby. Why, wassup?"

"Do you know a chick named Andrea?"

"Andrea Palmer?"

I try not to show my excitement. "Yeah, I think that's her last name."

"Hell yeah, I know her. Why, is that your homegirl or something?"

The way he says it and looks at me gives off the impression that being friends with Andrea is a deplorable act. *Only if I would've known.*

"I'm not gonna say we're friends. Really, we just worked together."

"Oh yeah, she did work up there, didn't she?"

"That's why I'm looking for her. The bitch borrowed some money, and when it came time to pay, that shooting happened and she disappeared."

"I heard about it. They say the laws are looking for her baby daddy, AD."

"Her baby daddy? I don't know him." I play dumb.

"You probably wouldn't. He's in the streets tough," he tells me.

Obviously, he's mistaken me for one of those suburban white girls who claim they love street niggas but are too scared to be in the trenches with them. I don't correct him, so he continues.

"AD's down with them Shark niggas, Savage Hustlers and Real Killas. I don't know if he smacked ole boy, but if he did, I'm not surprised."

"Well, I'm looking for Andrea so I can get my bread back, but I don't know where the bitch is at."

"Last time I checked, she was in Deerwood Pines off Maxey Road. I'll take you by there real quick," he offers.

We make the detour and head over there. When we get to Deerwood, I can tell the apartments have had a huge makeover.

"Her and AD stay in the back," he tells me as we maneuver through the complex.

When we pass a particular apartment, he points and says, "She stays right there." I look around to see if I can spot her car. I don't see it. *She must be gone.* I snap a mental photograph, and Tori B and me head back out the same way we came.

The whole ride home, Tori's talking my ear off while I'm trying to devise a plan. Now that I have the info I need, I really don't have any other use for him. I have him drop me back off at my apartment and immediately forget about him. *Can you feel me breathing down your neck, Andrea? Your time is coming!* I jump in the shower and wash the day away.

Two days later, I'm parked in Deerwood, waiting. It's drizzling outside, but you still got D-boys out there getting it in. One of them in particular catches my eye, about five-ten, a hundred and eighty pounds, red skin, and long hair. I sit back and watch him serve fiends out of a laundromat for twenty minutes before I decide to get his attention.

As he crosses the front of my car, I flash my headlights at him. He stops and looks, assuming I'm a lick coming to score some dope. When he tries to pull up to my driver's side window, I motion for him to go to the other side and get in. The minute he slides into my car, his whole demeanor changes. He didn't expect to find a pretty white girl with long legs and a nice set of titties sitting in the parked car.

"Damn, wassup? I know you ain't over here to buy no hard, is you?"

"Oh no. Well… not that type of hard. I'm really over here looking for a friend of mine. Do you know Andrea?"

He looks at me suspiciously. I can tell he's reluctant to give up that type of information. *What if I'm undercover?*

I need to ease his fears, but how?

"You got some smoke?"

He reluctantly reaches into his pocket and produces a sack.

"How much?" I ask.

"Shoot me sixty, and you can have the rest of this."

I reach in my purse, pull out three twenties, and hand them to him.

"You smoke?" I ask once I have the weed.

"Yeah, I smoke. On the cool, that's my personal sack I just sold you."

"Okay, well let's blow one. I need to run to the store right quick. You know how to roll?"

"Hell yeah, I know how to roll. And that's a bet."

We head to the corner store. While I'm roaming the aisles for some munchies, I catch his slick ass buying a three-pack of Magnum condoms. *Someone thinks they're getting lucky tonight,* I muse to myself.

Once we get back to the apartment, I let him twist one up and we blow our wigs back. I learn his name is Keemar, and he's a Blood. I could tell he was young, but his ass is only twenty years old.

"Why you looking for Andrea?" he finally asks, blowing pungent smoke through his nose.

"To be honest, she owes me money," I lie. I figure a dude from the streets who hustles can identify and sympathize with that the most.

He nods. "Well, I haven't seen her in a few weeks. Some people say they've seen her come home a couple times, grab some shit, and leave right back out the door. How much does she owe you?"

"Fifteen hundred."

Keemar makes a whistling sound. "I'm not even 'bout to ask for what. You can shoot me your number, and if I see her, I'll call."

Well played, lil' dude.

I give him my number, and we blow another blunt. By the time that blunt is down to a doobie, I'm high as fuck. I can't think straight. I lean back in my seat, close my eyes, tilt my head, and drift for a moment. Suddenly, I feel a hand rubbing against my thigh, inching closer and closer to my kitty. I didn't intend on fucking the lil' dude, but the weed has me on *fuck it* mode. His fingers find the warm patch of fabric protecting my goodies. I don't know how he plans on getting my shorts off, but if he can without my help, he'll get as much pussy as he can handle.

Suddenly, my phone rings. I open my eyes, and Keemar falls back, like he doesn't want me catching his hands in the cookie jar. I pick it up and see it's *Tori B.* I almost let it go to voicemail, but something tells me I should answer.

"Hello?"

"Kelsey, I got some good news."

"Talk to me." I'm so high, it takes all my energy to form words.

"I found Andrea."

My high instantly dampens. "What? Where?"

"I was heading to my plug's spot to score when I saw her leaving with some Mexican chick. I asked my plug about the female with the Mexican chick, 'cause I ain't want to raise no red flags, just in case the Mexican chick was his girl or something. He said she was his sister's girlfriend. The way he said it, I think Andrea's dyking now."

I can't believe it. She's always been bi, but to give up dick completely. *No way.* Now I'm eager to talk to him face-to-face. Tori B's stock just went up.

"Where you at?"

"I'm going through the tunnel right now."

"Okay, well meet me at the Burger King on I-10 and Federal."

"Bet!"

We hang up, and now Keemar's looking at me with a dejected expression.

"I gotta go, baby boy, but we'll definitely link up soon."

It seems like that's my favorite line these days. He looks like he wants to persuade me to stay, but I hit the locks on my doors to let him know ain't shit shaking. Five minutes later, I'm pulling into the Burger King parking lot. Tori has already parked, waiting. I hop out and jump in his whip. After he repeats what he said over the phone, I make him take me to the plug's house.

It's a little nondescript spot in Pasadena. If you didn't know any better, you'd think the house was vacant. We circle around twice before heading back to my car. Already, a plan is formulating in my head.

When I make it back home, I call Keemar. "Say, you tryna make some money?"

"Hell yeah. What's the play?"

I go ahead and tell him my plan. By the time I get off the phone, I can feel the trap closing around Andrea's neck. I won't stop until it snaps shut.

Chapter 13

Danielle

Damn, it's already four o'clock. I need to get my fat ass up and cook dinner. My baby Sosa usually likes to drop by the house for a quick meal and some top before heading back out in them streets. We've been together for two months, and I'm loving every minute of it.

Three weeks after we started fucking around, he asked me to quit my job and move in with him. I know a lot of people might be like, *bitch, you crazy,* but I need help, and if there's a big-dick-slanging, big-bag-having man willing to help, *fuck a job!* I'll let him take care of me. I wobble my eight-month ass into the kitchen to whip up something simple, spaghetti with sausage and shrimp. After the food's done, I call him to see where he's at.

"I'm just pulling in," he answers.

Perfect timing.

I make sure the front door is unlocked and lay back down on the sofa. I'm so big, nothing I wear can truly feel comfortable. I usually walk around the house in panties and a robe. Seconds later, Sosa Bay walks through the front door with a box of my favorite chocolates, a six-pack of Dr. Pepper, and a neck pillow. This man is *sooo* sweet.

Every time he steps through that door, he has something for me.

"Hey boo, how you feeling?" he greets.

"I'm good, food's on the stove."

"Yeah, it smells great. What is it?"

"Sausage and shrimp spaghetti."

"Bet, I'm starving."

He fixes a plate, eats, then washes the dishes. Later, he finds me in the living room, watching *The Voice.*

"That was delicious, baby. I'm really tempted to take some with me."

"Well, if you need to, go ahead. I already ate, so do you, baby."

He gives me a playful pout. "So you're not hungry? You sure?"

I catch his drift and smile. "Well, I do have room for dessert."

"That's my girl."

Sosa kneels next to my head and places a pillow under my neck for extra support. I pull at his waistband and out flops his dick. One thing about Sosa—he absolutely, positively loves getting his dick sucked.

Since we've been together, I've literally sucked his dick every single day. Each time, I've swallowed his nut down to the last drop. Today is no different. Never has his dick smelled like another woman's pussy, and he always comes with a full load. Just knowing I have a man that's completely mine is such a turn-on.

After Sosa floods my mouth with cum, he rubs my feet with baby oil. I stare at him with pure infatuation. In such a short time, I've fallen head over heels for him.

"Well, I'm 'bout to bounce, babe. I'll be back around three or four. Hopefully, you'll be up so I can get an early-morning snack before I head to bed."

He heads to the kitchen and fixes me a big cup of Dr. Pepper with crushed ice. He knows that's my favorite soft drink, and anything to prevent me from getting up, he's all for it. That's another one of our traditions, right before he leaves out, he'll fix me a drink.

Once Sosa leaves, I lay on the couch, sipping my soda and finishing my show. My mind starts to churn. I think about my past, and how I got to this point in life. I think about Kay. My heartbeat quickens. I think about my unborn son growing up knowing his daddy doesn't want anything to do with him.

Then, I think about my little sister Alison. I'm hearing rumors that she quit school, and her and Rah are fucking around. I don't believe it. She loves Chance's dirty drawers, and even though we've been beefing, I don't think Rah would stoop that low as to fuck my baby sister. Then again, he's been fucking his best friend/brother's longtime girlfriend, so…

I don't know what it is, but suddenly I feel like I need to get up and do something to occupy my mind. All that thinking has me depressed. I start cleaning up the living room, then I work on the bedrooms. After I'm done, I mop up the kitchen, and I still feel energetic. I throw on some loose-fitting joggers, a windbreaker jacket, and head outside for a walk.

Everything feels clear and focused. I realize that I truly love Sosa Bay and want to spend the rest of my life with him. After I've built up a sweat from walking around, I head back inside to take a shower.

As soon as I'm done, I step out dripping wet. A sharp, excruciating pain paralyzes me, it feels like a menstrual cramp times ten. I sit on the bed and try to compose myself. Suddenly, it stops. *Maybe I'm tripping,* I tell myself.

Just as I'm about to stand up and finish getting dressed, another one hits me, this time, even harder. I stumble toward my dresser drawer to grab a pair of underwear. I find some and pull them out, just as another crippling wave of pain rolls through me.

"Agggghhh, fuuuck!" I grit my teeth, grabbing hold of the dresser.

The panties fall to the ground. I bend over to pick them up, and a warm sensation cascades down my inner thighs. I look down to find a puddle of liquid at my feet. *My water just broke!*

"Oh no, no, no, no."

I frantically search for my phone. As soon as I find it, I hit Sosa Bay first.

"I'm on the way," he tells me.

I try to wait, but the contractions are unbearable. I notice spots of blood and start panicking. I call 911. Twenty minutes later, I arrive at the hospital and get wheeled into the delivery room. As I'm being prepped, the door opens and in walks Sosa Bay. My heart flutters at the sight of him. Suddenly, I feel like everything will be okay.

The doctor arrives, and I begin to push my baby boy out. Six hours later, we welcome Dominus Crowder to the world. I think I'll be able to hold him, but the nurse whisks him away. I feel drained, battered, and bruised. The nurse gives me a sedative, and before I know it, my eyes are closed. When I wake up, it's to a nightmare. In my room is a white woman in a navy-blue business suit, with an all-business demeanor. One of the nurses who helped deliver my son is also there.

"Where… where's my baby?" I ask, my throat hoarse from the strain of labor.

"Ms. Crowder, my name is Nancy Dzanski. I'm with Child Protective Services."

"What? C.P.S.? What's going on?"

"Well, your son was found to have methamphetamines in his system."

My heart drops. I shake my head repeatedly.

"No, no, no… there's gotta be some mistake. I don't even smoke cigarettes while I'm pregnant," I protest.

"Well, the blood work proves otherwise, and due to your negligence, the State will take custody of the infant until further notice."

Just like that, the bitch destroys my world and leaves, placing a card on the tray table before she goes.

"Ms. Dzanski, hold up. Please."

She turns around, clearly annoyed.

"How do I get my son back?"

"You'll have to go through the courts, but I will tell you this, judges don't look too fondly on mothers who ruin their kids' lives with drugs."

She then walks out, leaving me in total shock.

I can't breathe. I'm hyperventilating. *It's got to be a mistake.* I haven't done any drugs since I found out I was pregnant. My heart feels like it's been ripped out of my chest. I feel the judgmental stares of the nurse who was in my labor. I'm too afraid to speak.

As soon as she leaves, I let the tears come down. I'm so confused and helpless. The room door suddenly opens, and in walks my boo, Sosa. He sees me upset and rushes to my side, removing his customary shades.

"What's wrong, baby? I tried to go see lil' Dominus at the nursery, but they're talking about something dealing with C.P.S."

Having to tell him breaks the levee.

"They took him, baby. They took my baby boy," I howl. Snot bubbles out my nose as I cry uncontrollably.

"What? But why, baby? Why did they take him?" he asks, just as confused as I am.

"They're saying I have meth in my system."

Sosa looks at me perplexed. "Huh? Meth? But you don't even smoke."

"I tried to tell them,"I assure him.

"Well, don't worry, baby. We'll hire a lawyer and get this all figured out," he tells me.

I melt in his embrace. I'm so glad he's here, if he wasn't, ain't no telling what I'd be doing right now. I spend the next thirty minutes crying my eyes out until I'm so exhausted, I fall asleep.

Rah

"Damn, Alison, it's already *10:40 p.m.*, you still ain't ready?"

"Almost. I can't figure out what shoes I should wear, babe. You said this is a very important party with some very important people, so I want everything to be perfect."

"Well, if we don't ever make it to the motherfucka, what you're wearing won't even matter."

About two days ago, I got a call from Benji, inviting me to a very important get-together. He encouraged me to bring the *misses* with me, so of course, I told Alison. She's acting like she's more nervous about it than I am.

"Which shoes should I wear?"

"Well, considering you're wearing a white-and-black dress, I say rock the white Prada heels," I offer.

She considers my opinion for a second, then says, "Imma go with the black Bottega heels."

I shake my head, exasperated. "Well, whichever one you choose, your ass needs to come on."

"Okay, okay, I'm coming."

Alison disappears into the closet while I step outside to smoke me a cigarette. Ever since I met Benji at the club, I've been asking myself, *Should I take him down, or should I give this hustling shit a try?*

It's not that I can't hustle, I'm just lazy 'bout the shit. I don't wanna sit around all day, waiting on a nigga to hit my phone, when I can just wait for the next nigga to stack up and, in a couple minutes, take what he made in the last month. But now, with a plug like Benji, I can put a team together and have them hustle the shit for me. That'll free up my time to do other shit.

Just as I'm done with the square, Alison appears. "Ready?"

I look at her and smile. *Damn, lil' momma's a bad bitch.* She's got me wanting to bend her ass over, but we're already running late.

"Naw… is *you* ready?"

"Yes, Rah, let's go."

We hop in the car and head to the address Benji gave me earlier that day. About an hour later, we pull up to a two-story on an old country road. I honestly expected it to be a full-blown party, but it's more of a small gathering. About fifteen different exotic vehicles crowd the driveway and street. We park and head inside. I ring the doorbell, and a curvy Hispanic woman answers.

"Hey, how are you? Are you here for Benji?" she asks in a heavy accent.

"Yes," I respond, watching her turn and head back inside, clearly expecting us to follow. I can't help but stare at her ample backside swaying in that silk dress. Her long, reddish-brown hair flows down her back, tickling her ass crack. Alison smacks her lips, catching me ogling.

"What?" I say in defense.

She shakes her head but doesn't respond. The woman leads us into a living room where about twenty other people are grouped up, chatting and sipping drinks. Soon as we arrive, all eyes are on us. Benji's standing next to the fireplace, talking to another Hispanic man. *There sure is a lot of Mexicans in this bitch.*

He spots me and approaches with a warm smile. "Heyy, wassup, Rah. I'm glad you made it. I was starting to worry about you." I glance at Alison to let him know I wasn't the reason for our tardiness.

"You know I wasn't 'bout to miss it for the world,"I reply.

Benji takes one look at Alison and goes into mack mode. "And who is this lovely lady?"

"Oh, this my friend Alison."

I can tell by the way she flinches she doesn't appreciate the title, but she needs to understand, until I figure out if I'm gonna pluck him or not, I need to leave all options open. If he thinks she's just a friend, it'll be easier to use her as bait.

"Well, well, well. Nice to meet you, Ms. Alison. Would you like a drink?"

"Umm, sure."

Benji gives a head nod, and another woman appears, a white woman with blonde hair, blue eyes, and a nice lil' bubble butt.

"My friend Alexandria will show you where the drinks are at," Benji tells her. Alexandria leads Alison away, then he turns to me.

"Now that all the women are gone, let's discuss a little business."

I look around and realize I hadn't even noticed, all the women have somehow eased out of the room, leaving just us men.

"Rah, I've done a background check on you, and as far as law enforcement goes, you came back clean. I haven't heard your name associated with any major hustling, but that can be a good thing, so I won't hold it against you. My family and I are interested in opening up business in Houston, and we need some strong representation we can work through. What do you think you can handle starting off?"

"Well, to be honest, I haven't handled more than a few at a time, but if I have a steady supply, I'm pretty sure I can get rid of whatever you give me pretty quickly."

Benji nods, taking a few moments to think. "How 'bout we start you at twenty a month, see how that goes, and we'll bump it up."

I damn near want to jump for joy. For some odd reason, I think, *Damn, I wish Kaydon was here. That nigga would buss a nut behind getting twenty birds.* I play it cool, nod my head, and tell him, "I think we can do that. More than likely, I'll be done in less than a month."

"Well, if you do, I'll drop another twenty on you."

"Bet."

"Okay. Now that the first phase of business is concluded, let's seal the deal and have a lil' fun," Benji tells the crowd. I don't know what he has in mind, but *fuck it.*

"Can I see your car keys?"

"Huh? My car keys?"

"Yeah, your car keys."

I pull out my keys and hand them over. He places them in a large, empty fishbowl along with other sets of keys, then reaches in and mixes them up real good. I guess the look on my face warrants an explanation.

"This is what they call a key party."

"A key party? What's that?"

"Well, each one of us places our keys in the bowl. Then each one of the women will come out blindfolded and reach into the bowl for a set of keys. Whoever's keys they pull out, they spend the night with."

What the fuck!

The first thing I think is, *Damn, Alison ain't finna go for this.* I need to think of something fast. I'm not trying to have her fuck up my business deal.

"Oh shit, well I was unaware. I'm not sure my guest will be down with it… unless I can talk to her first."

"Understandable. Well, when she comes in to pick, I'll let you talk to her."

We stand patiently as the first woman comes out, led by the woman who answered the door. After she picks a set of keys, the owner takes her into one of the empty rooms in the house. The whole process takes less than a minute. Nervous excitement fills my body. Alison is the sixth woman to come out. Before she places her hand in the bowl, I approach her and whisper in her ear.

"Look, baby, I need you to play this game for me. I just struck a deal for us. It's very important we go with the flow. I'll explain later. Can you do that for me?"

She exhales, then nods. *I got you.*

I squeeze her arm in gratitude, then find my seat. She reaches in the bowl and pulls out a set of keys. *Benji's!*

Benji stands up, and jealousy rears its ugly head. The last thing I want is for my plug to be fucking my bitch. Anyone else wouldn't have been so bad, but not the nigga that's basically my employer. He grabs her hand and disappears with her.

My keys don't get picked until two women later. Surprisingly, it's the same woman who answered the door. I get up, grab her hand, and lead her to the back. Once inside, I remove the blindfold. She sees me and bites her bottom lip.

"I was hoping it was you," she admits.

"Oh yeah? Why's that?"

"You are a very sexy man, and I absolutely *love* Black men."

"You do?"

"Very much," she says, unbuckling my pants.

"How much do you love us?" I ask.

She drops to her knees, pulling my pants down in the process. I sit on the bed and let her show me just how much love she has for that Black dick. She grabs my piece with her small hands, licking the pre-cum off the tip.

"Let me show you."

With that, she shovels my cock into her mouth. I spend the next couple hours beating her back in. Her snatch is Super Soaker wet, and even with a condom on, it feels like a water balloon. She lets me put it anywhere I want, nothing is off-limits. We don't stop until the sun comes up. I leave her in the room asleep and head outside to the patio to smoke me a cigarette. Surprisingly, Benji's outside doing the same thing. When he sees me, he smiles.

"Did you have fun with Carla?" he asks.

"Is that her name?"

He laughs, obviously thinking I'm joking.

"Yeah, she was definitely something," I admit.

"Well, your friend Alison's definitely a spectacular piece of ass. If you haven't sampled her goods yet, you definitely need to."

A pang of jealousy bites at my heart, but I don't respond to that. Instead, I decide to pick back up on our earlier talks about business.

"What will you want back on those bricks?"

"Since it's consignment, bring me back five hundred. That's twenty-five a key."

"Bet, I'm cool with that."

"Plus, if you need artillery, my cousin's got guns by the truckloads. Anything you'll need—from pistols to rocket launchers."

"Fa' sho, I'll definitely need those."

Benji and I spend the next half hour hashing out the details. Suddenly, Alison appears looking worse for wear, hair disheveled, makeup smeared. *She looks like she's been through a hurricane.*

"Hey," I say smugly.

"Hey," she replies shyly.

"You ready?"

"Whenever you are," she responds.

I dap Benji up, and Alison and I head to the car. On the way home, I make an attempt at conversation, but her responses are cold, so I give up and we ride in silence. Whatever happened in that room must've fucked her up. I contemplate prodding a little further to find out, but then I think to myself, *maybe you don't want to know.*

Chapter 14

Demon

"Deb, I'm pulling up right now."

"Well, I'm not back yet, but Malvo's there."

I grit my teeth. It's not like I have something against dude specifically, I'm just not with getting buddy-buddy with a nigga that's fucking my sister.

"How long you gonna be?"

"Honestly, D, I don't know. Tracie just started doing my hair like a half hour ago. So, maybe another hour and a half."

"Well, look… I'mma just put this shit up, then bounce. I'll catch up with you on the flip side."

"Psshht. Why you gotta act like that? I don't get all bent out of shape about your lil' girlfriends. Every time one of my boyfriends come around, you act like you can't be around them."

"Deb, we already talked about this. I'm not 'bout to be getting all buddy-buddy with them niggas, 'cause if the time comes and I have to get active, I don't want nothing getting in the way, especially no bond I done built with one of these fuck niggas."

I've told her this a hundred times, but she still tries to get me to build relationships with these clowns.

"Okay, Damon, I guess I'll catch up with you when you come back to this side of town."

"Aight," I say before hanging up.

I pull up to her spot, grab my backpack, and head inside. I have a key, so there's no need to knock. I open the door and walk in. Malvo's sitting on the couch, no shirt, just boxers on. *Like he pays bills in this motherfucka!*

The nigga must've thought I was my sister, at first he jumps up to greet me, but once he sees who I am, he sits his ass right back down. I don't waste my breath speaking to him. Instead, I head back to my room, unlock the door, and go straight to my closet.

I have a safe bolted to the floor where I keep the bulk of my stash. I count out the cash and place it inside. According to my calculations, I have *$182,435* in there. I shut it and head back out the door.

Normally, I'd be worried about a nigga being in my sister's crib where I keep all my bread, but surprisingly, I'm not. I believe he knows, if he ever tried to steal from me, I'd blow his brains out the back of his head.

I walk past dude and head back outside. As I crank the car up and back out of the parking spot, I look up and see the blinds move, like he's watching me. *Weird ass nigga.*

Two days later, I'm out of town with Manny. This time, we're not burglarizing buildings, he's got the scoop on some out-of-town cats who supposedly push a lil' work.

We're in Tulsa, Oklahoma, parked down the street from a blue-and-white house, watching fiends come and go all hours of the night.

"What's the play?" I ask, gripping my MDX-PDX. That bitch spits 5.56 NATO's or 7.62's.

"This lil' bitch I fuck with says every morning that nigga Roscoe walks his daughter to school. We gone snatch both of them up, then make him walk one of us into the spot while the other holds down the lil' girl."

"So, who's doing what?"

"What you feel up to?"

"You know me, it don't make a diff," I reply, honest as ever.

"We'll flip a coin to see who gets all the fun."

"Aight, that's a bet."

Manny pulls a quarter out the ashtray. "Heads, you babysit. Tails, I do." He flips it, catches it. *Tails!*

"Damn… wanna do two outta three?" he tries to bargain.

"Hell naw, you got babysitting duties."

I check my watch, little after *6:30 a.m.* School should be starting soon. That's when a front door two houses down open, and a lil' mixed-breed girl steps out with a pink-and-black backpack slung over one shoulder.

"That's his daughter," Manny tells me.

"So, he stays a couple houses down from where the trap's at?"

"Yup."

I don't know if that's smart… or stupid. We watch as the lil' girl walks up to the trap and knocks. Seconds later, a dark-skinned, heavy-set man opens the door and scoops her into a hug. You can tell she adores her daddy. Once their greeting's over, they start heading down the street.

"Okay, so look, the school's about four blocks away. They'll have to make a left coming up. When they do, that's when we move. I'mma hop out and snatch the lil' girl up. That's gonna force him to comply. Once we get him in the car, we ride back over to the spot."

"Bet."

We park and lay in wait. Minutes later, Roscoe and his daughter make the turn. As soon as they pass the car, Manny hops out and snatches her from behind, his hand over her mouth so she can't scream.

Roscoe spins around, damn near dropping from shock and desperation, anger etched all over his face. He goes for the pistol on his waist.

"You do that and I'll kill her right here. Then my homie in the car will kill you," Manny warns.

Roscoe's eyes lock on me. Realization sets in. "What do you want? She's just a lil' girl."

"Yeah, I know. I ain't tryna hurt your precious princess. Me and my homie just want what's in your spot. Here's how it's going down, we all get in the car, head back over there. While I got your lil' girl, you're gonna walk my nigga inside and hand over all the dope and money. You try anything stupid, or I see any laws pulling up, Imma blow her head smooth off her lil' biddy shoulders."

He grits his teeth. "So once I give you the dope and money, you'll let my daughter go?"

"Of course. Ain't no reason to hurt her."

He thinks it over, but he knows he ain't got no choice. "Aight."

"Good. Good, daddy."

We load up, Roscoe in the front with me, Manny and the lil' girl in the back. When we pull up to the trap, I throw on a big black bubble jacket to hide my MPX. Before stepping out, Roscoe looks back at his daughter. "Don't be scared, Honey Bun. I'll be right back, okay?"

With Manny's hand over her mouth, she can't answer, just nods.

Roscoe and I walk to the door. I expect him to knock, but he pulls out a key, unlocks it, and walks right in. Immediately, I see two niggas in the living room watching TV. They glance at us, see Roscoe, then go back to what they're doing. *They must think I'm just a smoker he bumped into on the walk.*

"Snake, I need you to grab the rest of the work for me."

Snake gives him a look but doesn't question it. He gets up and heads to the back. My gut tells me letting him out my sight was a mistake, no way I can contain all three of them. One has to go… and it has to be now. I reach under my bubble, pull out my MPX, cock it, and press it to the head of the dude on the couch. He turns just as I squeeze.

Bocka!

His head explodes. Blood and bits of brain splatter against the TV screen. His body flops off the couch and onto the carpet. The unmistakable stench of metal fills the air.

"What the fuck? That was my cousin, man." Roscoe looks like he's about to cry.

"Fuck all that. Who do you love more, your cousin or your daughter? Where's the money and dope, and where the fuck is that nigga Snake?"

Roscoe starts trembling with rage. I put the stick to the back of his head. "Look, nigga, I'm not 'bout to go back and forth with you. Where the shit at?"

Reluctantly, he leads me to the back bedroom. Soon as we step in, I can see something's wrong, the window's wide open. *Fuck!* Snake must've jumped out. Either he sensed something, or Roscoe found a way to warn him. Ain't no telling what he's on his way to do. Could be bringing the cavalry back.

"Roscoe, where the fuck is the shit at?" I growl.

He doesn't budge.

Bocka!

I blow his left kneecap out.

"Aggghhhh!" he howls, hitting the floor.

"If I ask you again, the next one goes through your forehead. You saw what this bitch'll do to a skull. Now… where. Is. The. Dope. And. Money?"

"In the attic, man, fuck! It's in the attic."

I head to the hallway, grab the string, and pull the attic door down. I practically run up the ladder, searching for the loot. Finally, I spot a couple black trash bags. I grab them, heavy, full. I open one and see vacuum-sealed packs of money, dope, pills, and some Loud. I toss everything down, hop out the attic, and check the front window. So far, so clear. I think about finishing Roscoe, but the mission's the bread and butter. I tuck my stick under my coat; carry the bags out like I'm just taking out the trash.

Manny sees me and pops the trunk. Soon as I shut it, a black Monte Carlo comes speeding down the street. When it's about forty yards away, sticks start poking out the windows. *Fuck!*

I pull the MPX, up it, and let loose. *Pap, pap, pap, pap, pap!* Glass shatters, but they keep coming. I hop in the backseat as Manny peels off. Leaning out the window, I let my bitch bark. *Pap, pap, pap, pap.*

Shots whiz past my head as they return fire. *Bocka! Bocka! Bocka!* Manny cuts down a one-way into oncoming traffic. The Monte follows, but with the windshield shot out, they can't navigate worth a damn. They smash into a Ford Escort while Manny makes another sharp turn, then jumps on the freeway out of town.

My heart's pounding, sweat pouring down my face. *Damn, that was close as fuck.* Then I realize, we still got the girl. She's curled up on the floor, crying and shaking.

The plan was to grab the money and dope, then let her go. Now? I don't know. Manny's clocking seventy-five back toward Texas like she's not even here.

"M?... M?" I call him by his first initial.

"Wassup?" He turns, and when he sees what I see, he shakes his head. "Damn, I forgot she was in the car."

"What's the play?" I ask.

"Shit, we can't take her with us."

"Nigga, I know that. But what are we gonna do with her?"

He doesn't answer, just stares at me in the rearview. Our eyes meet, and the answer's clear. Manny exits the freeway. He knows the town well, 'cause before long, we're riding through a wooded area. The little girl's trembling, too scared to look at me. If I had to guess, she's eight, maybe nine. *Damn... this shit feels foul, but what else can a nigga do?*

Manny pulls into an abandoned park. Vines cover the swing sets and slides. Soon as he stops, the little girl starts crying harder. Then she's screaming, hollering for her daddy.

I gather my resolve, take the butt of the MPX, and whip her across the head. She goes out cold instantly, a huge knot rising on the top of her skull. I pull her from the car and carry her about thirty feet into the woods. Laying her on the ground, I raise my stick and steady my breathing.

As many bodies as I've caught, I've never killed a child.

I swallow the bile in my throat, aim the barrel at her frail little body, and squeeze. *Pap! Pap! Pap!* Her tiny frame doesn't stand a chance. When I'm done, she's unrecognizable. I shake my head in shame. *This one's gonna be hard to let go.*

After hopping back in the car, Manny and I don't speak for the rest of the ride. As soon as we cross into Houston city limits, my phone rings. It's my Uncle Lance.

"Wassup, Unc?"

"Where you at, D?" He sounds worried, frantic.

My hackles go up. "I was out of town, I'm coming in the city now. Why? What's wrong?"

"It's your sister."

"What?"

"She's in the hospital, D... and she's in real bad shape. Her eye socket's fractured, her jaw's broken, and two of her ribs are cracked."

My heart shatters, everything turns blood red.

"What happened?"

"We don't know the whole story yet, but some are saying it was her clown-ass boyfriend."

My hands shake. Pressure builds behind my eyes until it feels dangerous. I tell Manny to take me to my sister's crib. When I get there, what I see fucks me all the way up.

Claudia

"Oh, my gawd... oh my gawd... this dick feels soooo good,"I moan, as Kay sits back on the couch watching me fuck some random dude we picked up at the club. Now that the cat's out the bag, he knows exactly what I need, and he doesn't hold back. He treats me like the total slut I am. He's got me jacking dudes off in the corner of the club, letting different men finger-fuck me on the dance floor. But no matter what, I'm never allowed to cum. By the time this dude slides his dick between my meaty sex lips, I'm already about to buss my first nut of the night.

He's got me bent over, tooted up, dress bunched around my waist. Both titties out, panties pushed to the side. I stare into Kay's eyes as the stranger beats my box loose. The way he's staring back into my soul has me on the edge. But I can't.

I have strict orders not to cum until he tells me to. I bite my bottom lip so hard, I taste blood. My body starts to seize. My orgasm's pounding on the door of my pussy. I clutch the sheets, trying to hold it off. My eyes beg, plead, for release.

I shut them tight. I don't know how much longer I can hold on. My stomach muscles lock up. I open my eyes, and Kay gives me what I crave more than anything in the world right now, *release.*

He nods and strokes his chin. *The signal.*

I open my mouth wide, but no words come, only a feral howl as I have the most intense sexual phenomenon of my life. My chocha explodes. I can literally hear myself skeeting and squirting all over dude. A low, whiny sound, like a wounded deer, slips from my throat. I collapse, then black out. When I come to, dude's gone, and Kay's sitting next to me, stroking my face.

"Heyy, daddy," I greet him, eager to please.

"Hey… I thought you died on me," he jokes.

"If I did, I'd have died a happy woman." I reach for his zipper, pull him out. Lately, he's been all about bringing me pleasure, indulging my fetishes, even if it means going home with a dry dick. *Well... not tonight.*

Once I free him from his prison, I take him in my mouth. Slow at first. Sensual. I love Kay, and I want to make love to every part of him. I cup his balls, rolling them between my fingers while he runs *his* fingers through my hair, intertwining the strands between his thick, long digits. He grips the back of my skull, forcing me to take more of him. I let him in, deeper and deeper, down my throat. My airway's clogged, but fuck it, I don't let up. I push and push. Pubic hairs tickle my lips, but the grand prize still eludes me. I pull back, half an inch short of a full deep throat. He moans his approval, and I feel my clit start buzzing again.

Kay and I make love for two and a half hours straight. Once he stuck his dick in, I don't think we let it breathe. Even when we switched positions, I kept him inside me. When he cums, I make him fill me up, then plug me up until his dick gets back hard again. When it's time to go our separate ways, I want to cry. I've fallen head over heels for my husband's brother, and I honestly don't know what to do. I head home exhausted, sore, and well-sated.

My plan is to shower, but when I see that king-size bed, I strip butt naked and fall into it like a swimming pool. Harrell isn't due back for a while, so I figure I'll take a quick nap. Well… a while comes a lot quicker than expected.

"Claudia! Claudia!" I'm violently yanked from sleep by a rough pair of hands. I peel my eyelids open to see Harrell standing over me, a menacing scowl on his face. My mind's trying to warn me something's wrong, but my brain's still on vacation.

"What the fuck is this?" He's holding my panties in his hand.

"My panties," I reply dumbly.

"Yeah, I know. But I'm talking 'bout *this*." He shoves them in my face so I can get a closer look. Caked up in the crotch is a huge, dried-up spot of cum.

Oh fuck! Kay's cum must've been oozing out of me on the way home.

I look up at Harrell, scrambling for an explanation. But all I can think is, *where's my gun?*

Chapter 15

Andrea

My phone rings for the fifth time in thirty minutes. Without looking, I know exactly who it is… *Mary.* She's been blowing me up for hours, but I'm occupied, and it's hard to talk with a big-ass dick stuffed in your mouth.

For the last couple days, I've been rediscovering my love for cock. Ever since I saw Willie at the Galleria, he's been jumping up and down in my pussy. Fucking with him reminded me, *Andrea Palmer can't live without dick. No way.*

Right now, we're at the Omni. Willie's sitting on the edge of the bed, I'm on my knees with his big ole thing in my hands, stroking it slow, feeling him grow inch by inch.

"Damn, boy… I've missed this big-ass dick," I admit. It's not just the size, this man knows how to use it.

Some niggas blessed with big dicks feel the need to power-drive a bitch into the ground. That works sometimes. But most of the time, you can have a woman cumming in buckets if you ease up, give it to her in portions, gradually.

Willie knows exactly how to do that. By the time he's slamming into me balls-deep, I've already came three or four times. My coochie's well-lubricated and wide open for him. We've been going at it for hours, but I want to taste his cum one more time. This man's got the kind of dick that makes a bitch crave to swallow his kids.

"Ssshit, Drea… I don't remember you being this dick-hungry,"he points out.

"It's been a while… and I really, *really* miss your ass," I say, before taking him into my mouth.

"Sssshhhit," he hisses, as I work my neck, cupping his sack with both hands while bobbing my head on his pole.

"Fuuuck! Damn, girl… you gon' make a nigga fall in love with your ass."

Ghulp. Ghlup. Ghlup. Ghlup.

That just makes me go harder on the dick. I love the power I have over a man when he's at my mercy like this, controlling his pleasure. Willie starts grunting, humping his hips into my face, urging me to speed up.

"Oh shit… oh shit… I'm finna nut, Drea. Damn, bitch, you 'bout to make a nigga cum again."

I jiggle his balls, and before long, I feel them twitch and jump in my hand. His dick spasms, and sweet dick milk floods my mouth again.

"Mmmmmm." I moan around his shaft as he unloads it all. Once my mouth is completely swamped, I swallow him down with a smack of my lips and a kiss on his tip.

I release Willie and let his dick fall. He's still hunched over, gripping the sides of my head, huffing in my ear, clearly drained of energy. *Sensitive to the touch.*

Once he recuperates, I tell him to drop me off at my apartment. Since I started back fucking with Willie, I've been coming back to my place more and more. I'm technically staying with Mary, but I didn't want to walk into her accusing, suspicious eyes. I really do care for her, but maybe if she's willing to bring a man into the relationship, it might work. I just know there's no way I can live off just a pussy diet.

As we pull into my apartments, I make a decision, *I'll just tell her the real.* Better to get it out in the open now than later.

"So, when will I see you again?" Willie asks as he parks.

"Well, I don't know… when do you wanna see me again?"

He thinks for a second. "How 'bout tonight?"

"Damn, nigga… you ain't gon' give a bitch no time to snap back, are you?"

He laughs. "Hell naw. I need that cat to fit me like a glove."

"Boy, your ass is too much. Tonight it is."

I go to open the door, but he stops me.

"Drea?" I turn.

"I know you got a baby daddy *and* a girlfriend, but I'm really tryna see where we can take this."

Oh shit, not another one. Why does everyone wanna lock me down? Don't they know Andrea Palmer is a rolling stone?

"Look, Willie… I fucks with you the long way. I got a lot going on, and I don't wanna make promises I can't deliver on. Let's just keep doing what we're doing and let things grow organically. If it's meant, it's meant."

I grab the door handle, but again, he stops me.

"Okay, I can dig that. I know you got a lot going on, and I respect that. Just… give it some thought," he practically begs.

I can see it in his eyes, Willie has it bad for me. I don't blame him. I'm a bad bitch with a mean sex game. I know how to make a man feel like a king when I'm with him. Of course they'd want a woman like me in their lives.

I exhale before answering. "Okay, Willie… I'll think about it. But if we do lock in, I don't wanna hear about the baggage later."

He smiles while crossing his heart. "Cross my heart, hope to die."

"Boy, your ass is silly."

As I pull on the door handle, a black SUV comes whipping into the lot, driving sporadically. *Urrrgghhh.* They skid to a stop.

Three Mexicans with guns hop out.

"What the fuck?" Willie mumbles next to me.

We watch them head straight to my apartment and kick the door in. *What the fuck!*

"Ain't that your apartment?" Willie asks stupidly. I don't respond, just watch intently. *What the hell is going on?*

I grab my phone and scroll through my messages.

Mary: *How could U*Mary: *Grimy ass BITCH!!!*Mary: *You're gonna pay for that!*Mary: *You're dead*

I turn to Willie. "Let's get the fuck outta here."

He doesn't waste a second. As he backs out of the parking spot, one of the Mexicans comes out of my crib and spots me.

Emmanuel! He yells at his homeboys, and they come running outside.

"Willie, we need to go. NOW!" I scream, panicking.

Emmanuel and his boy jump in the black SUV just as Willie turns onto Maxey Road. As we near the freeway, I look back, they're hot on our trail.

"Fuck! We need to lose them," I scream.

"Drea, what the fuck is going on? Who are them Mexican niggas?"

"Willie, listen to me, I don't know what's going on, but if they catch up to us, we're both dead."

He looks at me, terrified. "Fuck!" he yells in frustration as we take Emmanuel and his boys on a high-speed chase.

Kay

"Kay, wassup. My pops called and said Chucho's back in the U.S. Me and Bro will come back to help you take care of that."

"Naw, naw… y'all good. I need y'all to stay put, keep doing what you're doing. The foundation must be laid so we can build the empire. I'll take care of Chucho myself."

I'd gotten the call about Chucho a few nights ago. He's back in the States and isn't too happy about Hector and his brother moving back on his territory. I've spent the last few nights getting intel on him. He's not one to have a bunch of niggas around, either he's solo or rolling with one of his top guys.

Chucho ain't a big man. About five-ten, one-ninety-five. Long hair tied in a ponytail. Got a gut but still fit for his size. I honestly don't know if I can take him down alone, but I gotta try. The mission I got the brothers on is too important to abandon. I met up with Hector three hours ago. He just flew in from Atlanta and wants to be in the city when Chucho goes down. *Guess even cartel members wanna flex when it's time to get rid of an op.*

I pull up and park the dopefiend rental, a black, tinted-up 2005 Chevy Impala with a dull paint job. I check my watch. *8:15 p.m.* I spark a Newport Short while scoping the taco stand Chucho hits every night.

All types of people pull up to get served, but what catches me is how many look like D-boys. Each one leaves with a bag big enough to feed a whole family. *They gotta be trapping out this bitch.*

Then a maroon dually pickup pulls up and parks. I sit up. *Chucho.* He hops out and heads toward the taco stand, but instead of going to the service window like everybody else, he slips through the side door.

Through the window, I watch him talking to the workers. I grip my Ruger AR-556, waiting. Surprising a big cartel boss don't roll heavier. I steady my breathing, can't afford to miss. Chances like this don't come twice.

Chucho finally looks like he's about to come out. I wait for the perfect moment, too soon or too late can both be deadly. But right before he hits the door, his phone rings. He answers, looking animated.

That's when another car pulls up and parks next to his truck. Two more Mexicans hop out. *Fuck.* This just got ugly. I pray they're just customers, but that's dead once I see the three of them converge in conversation.

My anxiety spikes. Three-on-one ain't what I was planning. I was gonna wear a mask, but there's no way to get the drop like that now. I leave it on the passenger seat and step out with my pistol concealed.

As I approach, I pull some money out. One of the Mexicans clocks me but don't see me as a threat. I order enchiladas and Spanish rice.

The woman behind the counter catches me eyeing Chucho. Her brows knit, and I can tell she's about to say something. I turn away, reach under my jacket, then she screams, *"CHUCHO!"*

He turns to her at the same moment I come up with my rod. *Bocka! Bocka! Bocka! Bocka!* One of the Mexicans shoves Chucho out the way and basically jumps in front of the bullets. The .556s connect, blowing his shoulder clean out the socket and spinning him to the ground. Screams erupt.

Chucho and the other Mexican duck back inside. I don't follow through the door, I dump through the service window instead. *Bocka! Bocka! Bocka!* Glass shatters. The woman at the register hits the floor in fright. I hop over the counter and land right above her. She looks up at me in fright.

"Please, mi have four kids."

Bocka!

I knock her noodles all over the tiles. Out the corner of my eye, I spot someone running back toward the side door. *Chucho!* Before I can chase him down, *Bocka! Bocka! Bocka!*, bullets whiz by my head, inches from bussin' my melon open. I duck, but instead of coming all the way up with the pole, I sweep low at knee level.

"Aggghhh!"

One of the Mexicans falls forward, leg bent outta shape, torn apart above the shin. I don't waste time finishing him. I hop back over the counter and catch Chucho getting into his truck, trying to get away.

Pap! Pap! Pap! Pap! Pap!

I don't let off the trigger. Glass shatters. Headlights explode. The engine starts smoking.

Pap! Pap! Pap! Pap!

I keep walking him down.

As I get closer, I peek over the dashboard into the truck. Chucho's a bloody mess, pieces of his torso missing, body shivering and shaking. I look to my left, and what I see fucks me up.

In the passenger seat is a boy.

Strapped in, tiny hands gripping his neck as blood pours between his fingers. *Fuck. Fuck. Fuck.* Where the hell did he come from? His eyes lock on mine, pleading for help. With his trachea destroyed, he can't speak.

For a second, I think about trying to help. *What the fuck is wrong with you, Kay?* This is war, he's just a casualty.

I shake off the guilt and run back toward the car. As I peel off, I call Hector and tell him everything. He's overjoyed to hear Chucho's dead.

"Why you ain't tell me about his son?"

"Huh? Chucho no have son."

"Well, there was a lil' nigga in the truck with him. Got his throat blown out."

Hector goes quiet. *"Let me make call, see what's going on."*

"Yeah," I reply, irritation boiling at the misinformation.

I drive the dopefiend rental into a field, douse it with gasoline, and set it on fire. Then I hop in my truck and head home. My phone vibrates—a missed call from Claudia.

I think about the last time we were together. Had her fuck some random nigga we met at the club. Finding out just how much of a freak she really is… unsettling. I don't think one man is enough for her. At the same time, she's made me realize things about myself. I didn't know how much I enjoy dominating a woman, owning her in every way.

As I turn down my street, I pass Nichanor and Tianna's crib, thinking about what she told me the last time she visited. I hop in the shower, wash the day away, and try to sleep… but every time I close my eyes, I see that little boy clutching his neck.

I get up, pour a stiff shot of Cognac to drown the guilt. Before I know it, I'm out cold.

Boom! Boom! Boom! Boom!

What the fuck?

I jump outta bed, thinking the police must be downstairs. I peek through the blinds only see Hector's Ram truck parked out front. I throw on some shorts and open the door.

He barges right in. "Kay, bro… we have problem. Mucho problem."

"Huh? What you talkin' 'bout?" He's moving around the house frantic. I've never seen Hector this shook.

"That boy you killed… not Chucho's son."

The way he says it, I already know it's some bullshit.

"Okay… so who was it?"

Hector drops his head, shaking it side to side. "Kay… you killed Jeffe Carlos' boy."

"Jeffe Carlos? Who's that?"

He looks at me like I'm slow. "Jeffe Carlos is the boss of Cartel de Muerte."

"But that's your cartel. What was his son doin' with y'all's rival?"

Hector finally sits, pinching the bridge of his nose like he's tryna keep from snapping. "Look… before I caught charge, me and Nichonar was over whole Southwest region. When I go to jail, Carlos feel I liability. He put Pancho and Chucho over mi territory."

Now it's all starting to make sense. That's why Hector needed me to take care of Pancho and Chucho, *because they're on the same team.* The hit wasn't sanctioned.

Getting a Black guy to do it:1.) Deflects attention away from them, and2.) Once they're dead, Hector and his brother can move back in on the territory.

"Okay, so what's next?" I ask.

"I don't know. They say Carlos come up to States next week. He want answers. You need to lay low for a lil' while."

"For what? Don't nobody know I did it but us, I—"

The look Hector gives me makes me pause.

"What?" I press.

"One of Chucho's bodyguards survived. He tell Jeffe Carlos everything."

My mind flashes back to the Mexican I shot in the leg. I curse myself for letting him live. I should've finished him. But then again, Chucho would've gotten away… and the boy would still be alive though.

I sit down, trying to compose my thoughts. Suddenly, Hector's phone rings.

"Hola? Huh… shit!"

I glance his way, his eyes get big as saucers. Whoever's on the other end keeps feeding him bad news.

"Sí… sí… okay."

When he hangs up, I feel it before he even says it.

"What?"

"Change of plans. Jefe Carlos isn't coming next week… he came now. His plane just landed. He wants to speak with me."

"When?"

"Now."

To be continued…

Lock Down Publications and Ca$h Presents Assisted Publishing Packages

Due to an increase in the price of services we have increased our prices. The prices below reflect the price increase as of 11/1/24.

<table>
<tr><td>BASIC PACKAGE
$699
Editing
Cover Design
Formatting</td><td>UPGRADED PACKAGE
$1000
Typing
Editing
Cover Design
Formatting
Upload eBooks to Amazon
Upload Paperback to Amazon</td></tr>
<tr><td>ADVANCE PACKAGE
$1,400
Typing
Editing (line editing/content)
Cover Design
Formatting
Copyright Registration
Proofreading
Upload eBooks to Amazon
Upload Paperback to Amazon</td><td>LDP SUPREME PACKAGE
$1,700
Typing
Editing (line editing/content)
Cover Design
Formatting
Copyright Registration
Proofreading
Set up Amazon Account
Upload eBooks to Amazon
Upload Paperback to Amazon
Advertise on LDP's Amazon and Facebook Page</td></tr>
</table>

***

Other services available upon request.
Additional charges may apply

Lock Down Publications
P.O. Box 944
Stockbridge, GA 30281-9998
Phone: 470 303-9761
Email: lockdownpublications@gmail.com

Submission Guideline

Submit the first three chapters of your completed manuscript to ldpsubmissions@gmail.com. In the subject line add **Your Book's Title**. The manuscript must be in a Word Doc file and sent as an attachment. Document should be in Times New Roman, double spaced, and in size 12 font. Also, provide your synopsis and full contact information. If sending multiple submissions, they must each be in a separate email.

Have a story but no way to send it electronically? You can still submit to LDP/Ca$h Presents. Send in the first three chapters, written or typed, of your completed manuscript to:

LDP: Submissions Dept
P.O. Box 944
Stockbridge, GA 30281-9998

DO NOT send original manuscript. Must be a duplicate. Provide your synopsis and a cover letter containing your full contact information.

Thanks for considering LDP and Ca$h Presents.

NEW RELEASES

BLOODLINE OF A SAVAGE 1-3
THESE VICIOUS STREETS 1-3
RELENTLESS GOON 1-3
BY PRINCE A. TAUHID

THE BUTTERFLY MAFIA 1-3
BY FUMIYA PAYNE

A THUG'S STREET PRINCESS 1&2
BY MEESHA

CITY OF SMOKE 3
BY MOLOTTI

GET IT IN SLUGS 1 &2
BY B. STALL

STANDING ON HER BUSINESS 1&2
BY DG SANTANA

STEPPERS 1,2&3
THE REAL BADDIES OF CHI-RAQ
BY KING RIO

THE LANE 1&2
BY KEN-KEN SPENCE

THUG OF SPADES 1&2
LOVE IN THE TRENCHES 2
CORNER BOYS
BY COREY ROBINSON

TIL DEATH 3
BY ARYANNA

BACK IN BLOOD 2 | LO-LIFE

THE BIRTH OF A GANGSTER 4
BY DELMONT PLAYER

PRODUCT OF THE STREETS 1-3
BY DEMOND "MONEY" ANDERSON

NO TIME FOR ERROR
BY KEESE

MONEY HUNGRY DEMONS 1-2
BY TRANAY ADAMS

HUB CITY MENACE 1-3
BY J. WHITE

A THUGGISH PASSION 1&2
LAND OF DA HOOLIGANZ 1-4
KILLAZ ON STANDBY 1&2
BY IRA B.

FO'EVA ROLLIN 1&2
BY ASSA RAYMOND BAKER

THE LEVEL UP 1&3
BY LUXURY KING

Coming Soon from Lock Down Publications/Ca$h Presents

IF YOU CROSS ME ONCE 6
ANGEL V
By Anthony Fields

A THUGS STREET PRINCESS 3
By Meesha

CORNER BOYS 2
By Corey Robinson

THA TAKEOVER
By Keith Chandler

BETRAYAL OF A G 2
By Ray Vinci

SAVAGE FAMILY EMPIRE 1&2
SOULLESS GOON 1,2&3
THE DIRTY SIDE OF MONEY 1,2&3
By Prince

FOR MY ENEMY'S SAKE
AMBITIONS OF A SLIDER
FRESH OFF DA PORCH
By IRA B.

BY THE TRUCKLOAD 1-4
TIPPIN' THE SCALES 1-3
BAD BITCHES WIT GUNZ 3
PROBLEM SOLVED 2
By Christopher "Diesel" Hornezes

Available Now

RESTRAINING ORDER 1 & 2
By **CA$H & Coffee**

LOVE KNOWS NO BOUNDARIES 1-3
By **Coffee**

RAISED AS A GOON I, II, III & IV
BRED BY THE SLUMS I, II, III
BLAST FOR ME I & II
ROTTEN TO THE CORE I II III
A BRONX TALE I, II, III
DUFFLE BAG CARTEL I II III IV V VI
HEARTLESS GOON I II III IV V
A SAVAGE DOPEBOY I II
DRUG LORDS I II III
CUTTHROAT MAFIA I II
KING OF THE TRENCHES
By **Ghost**

LAY IT DOWN I & II
LAST OF A DYING BREED I II
BLOOD STAINS OF A SHOTTA I & II III
By **Jamaica**

LOYAL TO THE GAME I II III
LIFE OF SIN I, II III
By **TJ & Jelissa**

IF LOVING HIM IS WRONG…I & II
LOVE ME EVEN WHEN IT HURTS I II III
By **Jelissa**

PUSH IT TO THE LIMIT
By **Bre' Hayes**

BACK IN BLOOD 2 | LO-LIFE

BLOODY COMMAS I & II
SKI MASK CARTEL I, II & III
KING OF NEW YORK I II, III IV V
RISE TO POWER I II III
COKE KINGS I II III IV V
BORN HEARTLESS I II III IV
KING OF THE TRAP I II
By **T.J. Edwards**

WHEN THE STREETS CLAP BACK I & II III
THE HEART OF A SAVAGE I II III IV
MONEY MAFIA I II
LOYAL TO THE SOIL I II III
By **Jibril Williams**

A DISTINGUISHED THUG STOLE MY HEART I II & III
LOVE SHOULDN'T HURT I II III IV
RENEGADE BOYS 1-4
PAID IN KARMA 1-3
SAVAGE STORMS 1-3
AN UNFORESEEN LOVE 1-3
BABY, I'M WINTERTIME COLD 1-3
A THUG'S STREET PRINCESS 1&2
By **Meesha**

A GANGSTER'S CODE 1-3
A GANGSTER'S SYN 1-3
THE SAVAGE LIFE 1-3
CHAINED TO THE STREETS 1-3
BLOOD ON THE MONEY 1-3
A GANGSTA'S PAIN 1-3
BEAUTIFUL LIES AND UGLY TRUTHS
CHURCH IN THESE STREETS
By **J-Blunt**

CUM FOR ME 1-8
An LDP Erotica Collaboration

BACK IN BLOOD 2 | LO-LIFE

BLOOD OF A BOSS 1-5
SHADOWS OF THE GAME
TRAP BASTARD
By **Askari**

THE STREETS BLEED MURDER 1-3
THE HEART OF A GANGSTA 1-3
By **Jerry Jackson**

WHEN A GOOD GIRL GOES BAD
By **Adrienne**

THE COST OF LOYALTY 1-3
By **Kweli**

BRIDE OF A HUSTLA 1-3
THE FETTI GIRLS 1-3
CORRUPTED BY A GANGSTA 1-4
BLINDED BY HIS LOVE
THE PRICE YOU PAY FOR LOVE 1-3
DOPE GIRL MAGIC 1-3
By **Destiny Skai**

A KINGPIN'S AMBITION
A KINGPIN'S AMBITION II
I MURDER FOR THE DOUGH
By **Ambitious**

TRUE SAVAGE 1-7
DOPE BOY MAGIC 1-3
MIDNIGHT CARTEL 1-3
CITY OF KINGZ 1&2
NIGHTMARE ON SILENT AVE
THE PLUG OF LIL MEXICO 1&2
CLASSIC CITY
By **Chris Green**

A GANGSTER'S REVENGE 1-4
THE BOSS MAN'S DAUGHTERS 1-5
A SAVAGE LOVE 1&2
BAE BELONGS TO ME 1&2
A HUSTLER'S DECEIT 1-3
WHAT BAD BITCHES DO 1-3
SOUL OF A MONSTER 1-3
KILL ZONE
A DOPE BOY'S QUEEN 1-3
TIL DEATH 1-3
IMMA DIE BOUT MINE 1-6
DYING FOR LIKES
By **Aryanna**

A DOPEBOY'S PRAYER
By **Eddie "Wolf" Lee**

THE KING CARTEL 1-3
By **Frank Gresham**

THESE NIGGAS AIN'T LOYAL 1-3
By **Nikki Tee**

GANGSTA SHYT 1-3
By **CATO**

THE ULTIMATE BETRAYAL
By **Phoenix**

BOSS'N UP 1-3
By **Royal Nicole**

I LOVE YOU TO DEATH
By **Destiny J**

I RIDE FOR MY HITTA
I STILL RIDE FOR MY HITTA
By **Misty Holt**

LOVE & CHASIN' PAPER
By **Qay Crockett**

TO DIE IN VAIN
SINS OF A HUSTLA
By **ASAD**

BROOKLYN HUSTLAZ
By **Boogsy Morina**

BROOKLYN ON LOCK 1 & 2
By **Sonovia**

GANGSTA CITY
By **Teddy Duke**

A DRUG KING AND HIS DIAMOND 1-3
A DOPEMAN'S RICHES
HER MAN, MINE'S TOO 1&2
CASH MONEY HO'S
THE WIFEY I USED TO BE 1&2
PRETTY GIRLS DO NASTY THINGS
By **Nicole Goosby**

LIPSTICK KILLAH 1-3
CRIME OF PASSION 1-3
FRIEND OR FOE 1-3
By **Mimi**

TRAPHOUSE KING 1-3
KINGPIN KILLAZ 1-3
STREET KINGS 1&2
PAID IN BLOOD 1&2
CARTEL KILLAZ 1-3
DOPE GODS 1&2
By **Hood Rich**

THE STREETS ARE CALLING
By **Duquie Wilson**

STEADY MOBBN' 1-3
THE STREETS STAINED MY SOUL 1-3
By **Marcellus Allen**

WHO SHOT YA 1-3
SON OF A DOPE FIEND 1-4
HEAVEN GOT A GHETTO 1&2
SKI MASK MONEY 1&2
By **Renta**

GORILLAZ IN THE BAY 1-4
TEARS OF A GANGSTA 1/&2
3X KRAZY 1&2
STRAIGHT BEAST MODE 1&2
By **DE'KARI**

TRIGGADALE 1-3
MURDA WAS THE CASE 1-3
By **Elijah R. Freeman**

SLAUGHTER GANG 1-3
RUTHLESS HEART 1-3
By **Willie Slaughter**

GOD BLESS THE TRAPPERS 1-3
THESE SCANDALOUS STREETS 1-3
FEAR MY GANGSTA 1-5
THESE STREETS DON'T LOVE NOBODY 1-2
BURY ME A G 1-5
A GANGSTA'S EMPIRE 1-4
THE DOPEMAN'S BODYGAURD 1&2
THE REALEST KILLAZ 1-3
THE LAST OF THE OGS 1-3
By **Tranay Adams**

MARRIED TO A BOSS 1-3
By **Destiny Skai & Chris Green**

KINGZ OF THE GAME 1-7
CRIME BOSS 1-4
By **Playa Ray**

FUK SHYT
By **Blakk Diamond**

DON'T F#CK WITH MY HEART 1&2
By **Linnea**

ADDICTED TO THE DRAMA 1-3
IN THE ARM OF HIS BOSS
By **Jamila**

LOYALTY AIN'T PROMISED 1&2
By **Keith Williams**

YAYO 1-4
A SHOOTER'S AMBITION 1&2
BRED IN THE GAME
By **S. Allen**

TRAP GOD 1-3
RICH $AVAGE 1-3
MONEY IN THE GRAVE 1-3
CARTEL MONEY 1&2
By **Martell Troublesome Bolden**

FOREVER GANGSTA 1&2
GLOCKS ON SATIN SHEETS 1&2
By **Adrian Dulan**

TOE TAGZ 1-4
LEVELS TO THIS SHYT 1&2
IT'S JUST ME AND YOU
By **Ah'Million**

BACK IN BLOOD 2 | LO-LIFE

KINGPIN DREAMS 1-3
RAN OFF ON DA PLUG
By **Paper Boi Rari**

THE STREETS MADE ME 1-3
By **Larry D. Wright**

CONFESSIONS OF A GANGSTA 1-4
CONFESSIONS OF A JACKBOY 1-3
CONFESSIONS OF A HITMAN
CONFESSIONS OF A DOPE BOY
By **Nicholas Lock**

I'M NOTHING WITHOUT HIS LOVE
SINS OF A THUG
TO THE THUG I LOVED BEFORE
A GANGSTA SAVED XMAS
IN A HUSTLER I TRUST
By **Monet Dragun**

QUIET MONEY 1-3
THUG LIFE 1-3
EXTENDED CLIP 1&2
A GANGSTA'S PARADISE
By **Trai'Quan**

CAUGHT UP IN THE LIFE 1-3
THE STREETS NEVER LET GO 1-3
By **Robert Baptiste**

NEW TO THE GAME 1-3
MONEY, MURDER & MEMORIES 1-3
By **Malik D. Rice**

CREAM 2-3
THE STREETS WILL TALK
By **Yolanda Moore**

THE STREETS WILL NEVER CLOSE 1-3
By **K'ajji**

LIFE OF A SAVAGE 1-4
A GANGSTA'S QUR'AN 1-4
MURDA SEASON 1-3
GANGLAND CARTEL 1-3
CHI'RAQ GANGSTAS 1-4
KILLERS ON ELM STREET 1-3
JACK BOYZ N DA BRONX 1-3
A DOPEBOY'S DREAM 1-3
JACK BOYS VS DOPE BOYS 1-3
COKE GIRLZ
COKE BOYS
SOSA GANG 1&2
BRONX SAVAGES
BODYMORE KINGPINS
BLOOD OF A GOON
By **Romell Tukes**

CONCRETE KILLA 1-3
VICIOUS LOYALTY 1-3
BLOODY MONEY BAGS
By **Kingpen**

THE ULTIMATE SACRIFICE 1-6
KHADIFI
IF YOU CROSS ME ONCE 1-3
ANGEL 1-4
IN THE BLINK OF AN EYE
By **Anthony Fields**

THE LIFE OF A HOOD STAR
By **Ca$h & Rashia Wilson**

NIGHTMARES OF A HUSTLA 1-3
BLOOD AND GAMES 1&2
By **King Dream**

GHOST MOB
By **Stilloan Robinson**

HARD AND RUTHLESS 1&2
MOB TOWN 251
THE BILLIONAIRE BENTLEYS 1-3
REAL G'S MOVE IN SILENCE
By **Von Diesel**

MOB TIES 1-7
SOUL OF A HUSTLER, HEART OF A KILLER 1-3
GORILLAZ IN THE TRENCHES
OOPS CRY TOO 1&2
THE DAUGHTER OF A CARTEL BOSS
By **SayNoMore**

BODYMORE MURDERLAND 1-3
THE BIRTH OF A GANGSTER 1-4
By **Delmont Player**

FOR THE LOVE OF A BOSS 1&2
By **C. D. Blue**

KILLA KOUNTY 1-5
TENDER
By **Khufu**

MOBBED UP 1-4
THE BRICK MAN 1-5
THE COCAINE PRINCESS 1-10
STEPPERS 1-3
SUPER GREMLIN 1-4
A GANGSTA'S SON
By **King Rio**

MONEY GAME 1&2
By **Smoove Dolla**

BACK IN BLOOD 2 | LO-LIFE

A GANGSTA'S KARMA 1-5
By **FLAME**

KING OF THE TRENCHES 1-3
By **GHOST & TRANAY ADAMS**

BAD BITCHES WIT GUNZ 1&2
PROBLEM SOLVED
By "Christopher Diesel" Hornezes

QUEEN OF THE ZOO 1&2
By **Black Migo**

GRIMEY WAYS 1-3
BETRAYAL OF A G
By **Ray Vinci**

XMAS WITH AN ATL SHOOTER
By **Ca$h & Destiny Skai**

KING KILLA 1&2
By **Vincent "Vitto" Holloway**

BETRAYAL OF A THUG 1&2
By **Fre$h**

COUNTDOWN OF A KILLA 1&2
SEX, MURDER AND GOD 1&2
GUNS DOWN, BOTTOMS UP 1&2
By Lo-Life

THE MURDER QUEENS 1-7
By **Michael Gallon**

FOR THE LOVE OF BLOOD 1-4
By **Jamel Mitchell**

BACK IN BLOOD 2 | LO-LIFE

HOOD CONSIGLIERE 1&2
NO TIME FOR ERROR
By **Keese**

PROTÉGÉ OF A LEGEND 1,2&3
LOVE IN THE TRENCHES 1&2
By **Corey Robinson**

THE PLUG'S RUTHLESS DAUGHTER 1&2
By **Tony Daniels**

BORN IN THE GRAVE 1-3
CRIME PAYS
By **Self Made Tay**

MOAN IN MY MOUTH
By **XTASY**

TORN BETWEEN A GANGSTER AND A GENTLEMAN
By **J-BLUNT & Miss Kim**

LOYALTY IS EVERYTHING 1-3
CITY OF SMOKE 1-3
By **Molotti**

HERE TODAY GONE TOMORROW 1&2
By **Fly Rock**

WOMEN LIE MEN LIE 1-4
FIFTY SHADES OF SNOW 1-3
STACK BEFORE YOU SPLURGE
GIRLS FALL LIKE DOMINOES
NAÏVE TO THE STREETS
By **ROY MILLIGAN**

PILLOW PRINCESS
By **S. Hawkins**

BACK IN BLOOD 2 | LO-LIFE

THE BUTTERFLY MAFIA 1-3
SALUTE MY SAVAGERY 1&2
By **Fumiya Payne**

THE LANE 1&2
By Ken-Ken Spence

THE PUSSY TRAP 1-5
By **Nene Capri**

DIRTY DNA
By **Blaque**

SANCTIFIED AND HORNY
by **XTASY**

BOOKS BY LDP'S CEO, CA$H

TRUST IN NO MAN
TRUST IN NO MAN 2
TRUST IN NO MAN 3
BONDED BY BLOOD
SHORTY GOT A THUG
THUGS CRY
THUGS CRY 2
THUGS CRY 3
TRUST NO BITCH
TRUST NO BITCH 2
TRUST NO BITCH 3
TIL MY CASKET DROPS
RESTRAINING ORDER
RESTRAINING ORDER 2
IN LOVE WITH A CONVICT
LIFE OF A HOOD STAR
XMAS WITH AN ATL SHOOTER

www.ingramcontent.com/pod-product-compliance
Lightning Source LLC
La Vergne TN
LVHW020714110826
845149LV00012B/2259

9781971770239